AURORA OF TALES

COLLECTION OF NANO TALES

JYOTIDIP BARMAN

Dedicated to my sons Aparajito, Adwitiyo and family.

Also, an ode to Dida, Amma and Dadu.

May the stories serve as a testament to life and echo all conversation that gets lost in the daily commotion.

Also to the people who aspire to dream and achieve, no matter what the situation is.

Within the pages of our imagination lies the extraordinary tapestry of life. May life continue to weave your dreams into the fabric of reality, shaping a world of wonder and possibility as beautiful as the auroras.

Contents

Contents

Contents

Contents

Preface

Welcome, dear reader, to this collection of nano tales. Within these pages, let's embark on a journey through the myriad landscapes of human experience, where every tale is a glimpse into the kaleidoscope of life.

Here we capture moments, emotions, and truths in condensed form, inviting readers to immerse themselves in worlds both familiar and fantastical. Each story is a testament to the richness of human existence, a mirror reflecting the complexities of our hearts and minds.

In this collection, we will encounter characters who grapple with love, loss, hope, and despair. From the quiet intimacy of everyday conversations to the grandeur of extraordinary events, these stories explore the depths of human emotions with honesty and compassion.

Let's embrace the beauty and complexity of these narratives, to lose yourself in the rhythm of their prose, and to find moments of reflection and revelation within their pages. Whether you seek solace, inspiration, or simply a moment of escape, may these stories resonate with you and remind you of the boundless possibilities inherent in the human spirit.

As you turn the pages of this book, remember that each story is a whisper from the past, a echo of the present, and a harbinger of the future. May they linger in your thoughts long after you've finished reading, sparking conversations, igniting imaginations, and inspiring new dreams.

Acknowledgements

I would like to express my sincere appreciation to my sister, Rameswari Barman, for her invaluable contributions to the creation of this book. Her expertise in designing illustrations and editing the tales with precision and care played a crucial role in shaping the book.

I am truly grateful for her unwavering support and dedication throughout this journey.

PROLOGUE

In the quiet corners of our minds and the bustling streets of our cities, stories are born. They emerge from the depths of imagination, woven from the threads of memory, experience, and the whispers of the heart. These nano tales, like constellations in the night sky, offer guidance, solace, and illumination to those who dare to listen.

In this prologue, we embark on a journey into the realm of nano storytelling—a journey where the boundaries between reality and fantasy blur, and where the ordinary becomes extraordinary.

As we venture forth, let us cast aside our preconceptions and open ourselves to the magic of life.

For in these tales, we will encounter the essence of humanity—the hopes, fears, dreams, and struggles that unite us all.

So, let us set forth together into this world of wonder and imagination.

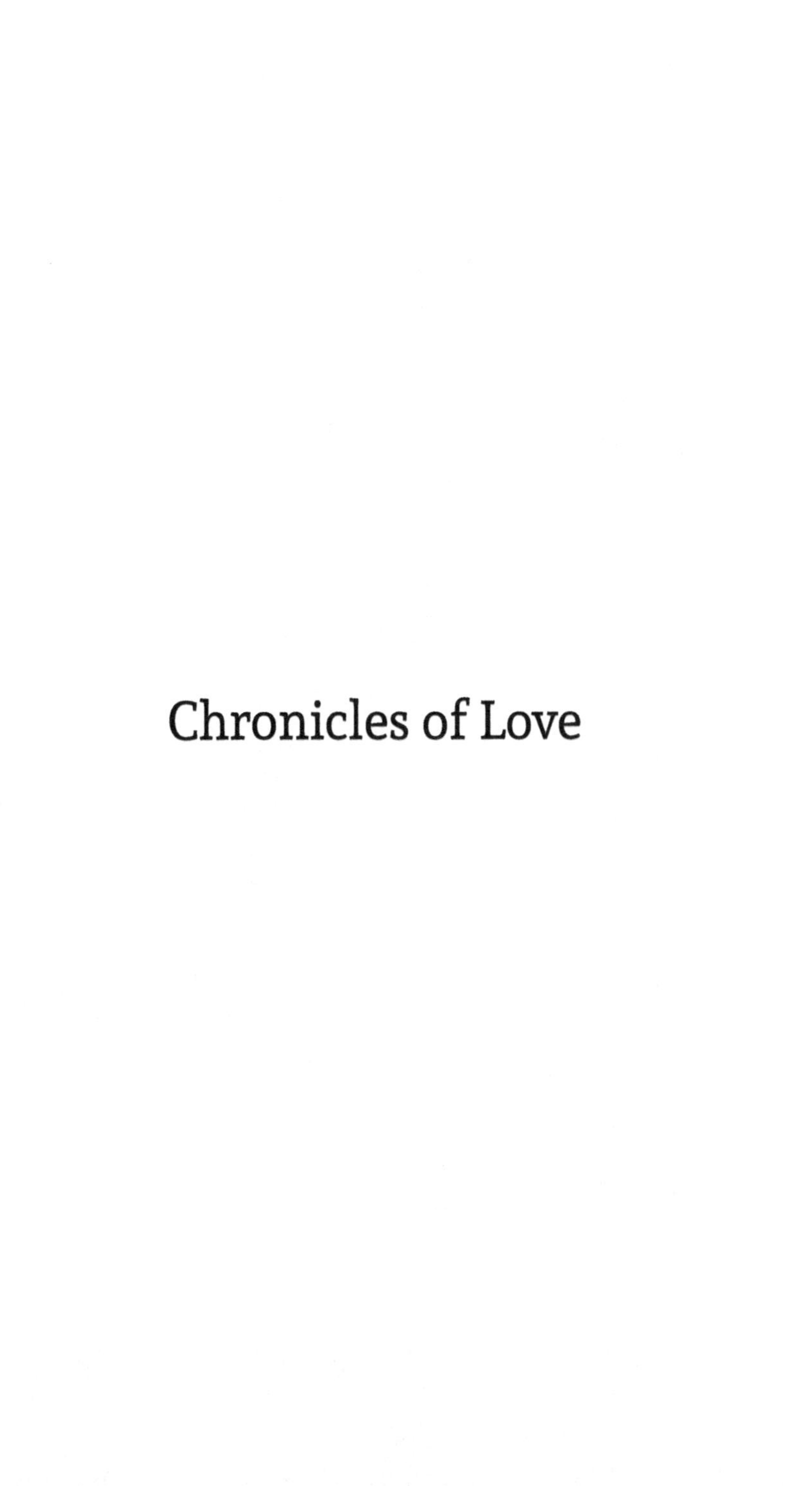

Chronicles of Love

I
One Love

Krishna found himself deeply enamored with Radha, the sister of his closest friend. And, intriguingly enough, Radha reciprocated his affection with equal fervor.

However, fate played a cruel hand. Radha's marriage was hastily arranged while Krishna was away, leaving him powerless to intervene.

Before Krishna could even contemplate his next move, the marriage vows had been exchanged, sealing Radha's fate with another.

Despite the unexpected turn of events, Radha endeavored to find contentment with her chosen life partner.

Meanwhile, Krishna's demeanor shifted. Once a steadfast lover, he now flits from one dalliance to another, eschewing thoughts of commitment.

Radha's rejection shattered Krishna's once-whole heart into myriad fragments, each harboring its longing for affection.

Indeed, the heart, a singular vessel for love, proves fragile. Once wounded or betrayed, its healing is a daunting endeavour, leaving one forever altered by the experience.

One Love is enough if its pure to be complete.

II
Second Love

An alarm shattered the stillness of the Ashiyana old age home in the early hours of Monday morning.

Divakar had vanished from Ashiyana without a word to anyone, leaving behind a void of unanswered questions.

Only one soul held the key to this mysterious disappearance: Maya, a fellow resident who shared a deep bond with Divakar.

Their love story had blossomed within the confines of the home, a beacon of hope amidst the solitude of aging.

Together, they had dared to dream of a new beginning, crafting plans for a shared future they dubbed "Second Innings."

Their desire to rebuild their lives, estranged from their families, fueled their resolve.

Yet, amidst their hopeful aspirations, a cruel twist of fate emerged: Divakar was afflicted with Alzheimer's, a cruel thief stealing memories.

Unaware of his condition, Maya remained steadfast in her belief that Divakar would return to her, unaware of his absence.

Alone and with no one to confide in, Maya clung to the flickering flame of hope, her heart yearning for the day Divakar would find his way back to her side.

For Maya, love transcended the boundaries of time and memory.

In its incompleteness lay the true essence of their bond.

If it ain't complete, it is love...

III

Best Couple

"... And the award for Best Couple in The Colony goes to... Mr. and Mrs. Roy from Ananda Vila Flat no 102..." The hall erupted in applause as Rohit and Sonia embraced each other, their joy palpable as they exchanged smiles and shook hands with well-wishers. The Chairman of the society proudly presented them with the prize.

Just three years earlier, the same couple had sat in a courtroom, their marriage on the brink of dissolution. Amidst the solemn proceedings, Sonia's tears betrayed the pain within, while Rohit, resigned to their fate, remarked, "So, it's over. Finally!"

Sonia met his gaze with a steely resolve, her voice trembling with suppressed emotion. "Yes. It is." As she rose to leave, a familiar touch on her hand halted her. Without looking back, she heard Rohit's plea, his words heavy with remorse. "Sonia! You know I'm terrible at making decisions. I was wrong, but this time, it's different. Please don't leave." Tears streamed down his face, a raw display of vulnerability that pierced Sonia's heart.

Overwhelmed by a flood of emotions, Sonia turned and delivered a resounding slap to Rohit's cheek. "STUPID!" But beneath the anger lay a profound longing for reconciliation. In an instant, their embrace dissolved the barriers that had threatened to tear them apart.

The applause echoing through the hall served as a poignant reminder of their journey—from the brink of divorce to the pinnacle of marital success. Their shining eyes bore witness to the enduring power of love and forgiveness.

• 7 •

IV
Mamma's Big Shopping Days

Pratik's mom is depicted as a tech-savvy individual, adept at handling smartphones, internet browsing, and WhatsApp chats. Her eagerness to explore shopping offers leads her to order a Designer Saree from an e-commerce site, opting for the "Cash On Delivery" option.

Upon receiving the saree, she discovers that it's not the red one she ordered but a white one instead. Her frustration is palpable, symbolized by her face turning red with anger. She promptly contacts customer care to initiate the return process.

Meanwhile, Pratik also purchases from the same e-commerce site, coincidentally encountering the same courier who had delivered the saree. The situation escalates when Pratik's mom confronts the courier, expressing her dissatisfaction with the wrong delivery.

Despite the courier's pleas to contact customer care, Pratik's mom insists on checking the courier's bag for her saree, leading to the courier fleeing the scene and returning the item to the warehouse.

Pratik becomes aware of the situation through an email alert and calls his mom, who criticizes him for ordering from the same site. He defends himself, highlighting that he had already paid for the item , and suggests she accept the delivery.

In an attempt to track the delivery, Pratik's mom bombards the courier with missed calls, prompting him to turn off his phone to avoid further confrontation.

V

Be Mine

The voice recording, lasting for 10 minutes, captures Soniya bidding farewell to her unrealistic love, Rohit, who is 10 years her junior.

Their relationship has been confined to messages and voice notes; they have never met in person. Despite initial doubts about its longevity, the allure of each call kept their unrealistic bond alive.

However, life's cruel irony unfolds as the narrative progresses. The illusion of their relationship shatters with Soniya's heartbreaking revelation of her battle with cancer. In her final message, she utters four words that encapsulate both despair and hope: "Be mine next life!!!!!!!!"

VI
Solitude

Amidst the overcast skies of a weekend, Rohit found himself entangled in a web of uncertainty. Morning obligations tethered him to his desk, yet his thoughts danced with anticipation of a rendezvous with Sonia, his heart yearning for the warmth of her presence, perhaps over dinner.

As the clock ticked, Rohit diligently completed his tasks, eager to embrace the moments that awaited him. However, as the minutes stretched into an hour after his return home, Sonia remained elusive, her absence casting a shadow over Rohit's plans.

Uncertainty gnawed at Rohit's mind, planting seeds of doubt. Could Sonia have crossed paths with Samar, her former flame? Memories of their history together lingered like ghosts in Rohit's thoughts, haunting him with the specter of insecurity.

Just as Rohit's imagination began to weave tales of betrayal, Sonia's call pierced through the fog of uncertainty. Her voice, tinged with distress, revealed her plight—stranded at Bally station amidst the onslaught of heavy rains.

Concern flooded Rohit's voice as he inquired about her safety and the state of the train lines. Yet, Sonia's response held an unexpected twist—a mention of Samar's presence alongside her, igniting a tempest of conflicting emotions within Rohit.

The call ended abruptly as Rohit grappled with the tumultuous whirlwind of his feelings. The weight of uncertainty bore down on him, echoing the timeless struggles of human relationships across centuries.

As the night deepened, Sonia found herself traversing the desolate expanse surrounding Chandernagar Railway Station, her steps echoing in the silent solitude of the night, a solitary figure amidst the chaos of her emotions.

VII

Last Goodbye

As the final day dawned for the B.Tech ECE 2008-2012 batch, emotions ran high as they gathered for a heartfelt farewell organized by their junior counterparts. Amidst laughter and tears, they made grand promises of eternal friendship and reunions, unaware of the unpredictable twists that awaited them in the years ahead.

Little did they know that their paths would diverge so drastically, as fate wielded its unpredictable hand.

Amit, with dreams of a life abroad, soared to new heights, securing a prestigious position as a Senior Engineer at IOCL, his accomplishments shining brightly.

Sayan's once-solid relationship with Meenakshi crumbled, leaving him grappling with heartbreak as she found solace with an NRI, forever altering the course of their lives.

Sukanta, once dismissed for his lack of academic interest, defied expectations by rising to the esteemed role of Head of Department at an engineering college, a testament to his resilience and determination.

Manami, a vocal advocate for women's empowerment, found herself navigating the complexities of motherhood, choosing to prioritize her family over her career aspirations, a decision laden with both sacrifice and fulfillment.

Meanwhile, many who once aspired to pursue Ph.D. degrees found themselves immersed in the demanding world of IT office campuses, their dreams taking unexpected detours.

In the wake of these divergent paths, the promises made during their last goodbye echoed hollowly, their resonance dulled by the harsh realities of life.

Yet, amidst the shattered dreams and altered priorities, there remained a glimmer of resilience—a steadfast determination to adapt and thrive in the face of adversity.

For in the ebb and flow of life's unpredictable currents, the true measure of friendship lies not in the promises made, but in the unwavering support and understanding that withstands the test of time.

VIII
Revenge

Smita has achieved a significant milestone in her journey by completing her MBBS degree at R.G. Kar Hospital in Kolkata and now works there.

This success was hard-earned, marked by three challenging attempts to clear the Medical Joint Exam. Each failure only fueled her determination to succeed.

During her rounds, Smita encounters a familiar face—a reminder of her past struggles. Three years prior, she had bravely pursued her dream of becoming a doctor but faced adversity when she encountered bullying and harassment during her nursing training. Forced to abandon her studies, she returned home, determined to prove her resilience.

With unwavering support from her family and relentless determination, Smita finally succeeded in her fourth attempt at the exam. Despite the naysayers who belittle her achievement, Smita's perseverance is a testament to her strength and courage.

Encountering one of her former tormentors, Sunita, now under her supervision, could have sparked bitterness and resentment. Instead, Smita chooses to respond with grace, offering a sweet smile and moving forward without seeking revenge.

In this tale of triumph over adversity, Smita's smile becomes a powerful symbol of resilience and forgiveness—a reminder that kindness can be more potent than vengeance.

As Smita continues on her journey, her story serves as inspiration for anyone facing challenges and setbacks. Her resilience, determination, and ability to rise above adversity embody the spirit of perseverance and hope.

Through Smita's journey, we are reminded that success is not defined by the obstacles we face but by our ability to overcome them with grace and resilience.

Emotional Odyssey

IX

Wish

As a volunteer at an NGO dedicated to serving underprivileged children, Rohit often found himself immersed in heartwarming initiatives aimed at bringing joy and fulfillment to young lives. One such initiative, "Make A Wish," offered children the opportunity to express their deepest desires, with the promise of the organization striving to fulfill them.

During one of these sessions, Rohit encountered a remarkable young girl named Brishti. As she returned her blank wish sheet, her solemn demeanor caught his attention. Sensing her reluctance, Rohit gently urged her to share her desire, prepared to tackle any request, no matter how grand.

However, Brishti's response left him speechless. Her wish was not for material wealth or extravagant possessions but for something far more profound—a mother. At that moment, the weight of her longing for a lost loved one brought Rohit to a humbling realization.

Reflecting on Brishti's wish, Rohit felt a profound sense of shame for his initial assumptions and trivial concerns. There was a young soul whose innocence had been overshadowed by profound loss, yet her wish remained a poignant reminder of life's true priorities.

In Brishti's simple yet profound wish, Rohit found a profound lesson—one that transcended material wealth and highlighted the importance of love, family, and human connection. It was a humbling reminder that, despite our best intentions, some desires cannot be fulfilled by mere monetary means.

Brishti's wish remains etched in Rohit's memory as a testament to the resilience and depth of the human spirit. In her innocence and vulnerability, she taught him a valuable lesson about empathy, compassion, and the true meaning of fulfillment.

As Rohit continues his journey of service and volunteerism, Brishti's wish serves as a guiding light—a reminder to approach every interaction with humility, empathy, and a genuine desire to make a meaningful difference in the lives of others.

X
Happiness

Rohit and his sister Priya embarked on a journey to their uncle's house on the eve of Christmas, opting for a rickshaw ride to reach their destination.

Upon reaching their stop, the rickshaw puller requested a slightly higher fare, sparking Rohit's ire. However, Priya's compassionate perspective reminded him of the rickshaw puller's humble circumstances, urging him to reconsider his reaction.

Swallowing his anger, Rohit apologized and offered extra money in penance for his outburst. Yet, the rickshaw puller refused the additional payment, asserting that he only sought fair compensation for his services.

Intrigued by the rickshaw puller's contentment, Rohit inquired about his occupation. The man proudly declared that pulling rickshaws was his sole profession, finding joy and fulfillment in his simple way of life.

Expressing gratitude for the man's wisdom, Rohit offered him a cake intended for his uncle and embraced him tightly. With heartfelt farewells, they parted ways, leaving Rohit profoundly touched by the rickshaw puller's perspective on true wealth and happiness.

In this brief encounter, Rohit learned a valuable lesson about the importance of gratitude, humility, and finding joy in life's simplest pleasures. Through the rickshaw puller's example, he discovered that true richness lies not in material possessions, but in the love and contentment found within one's family and community.

As Rohit and Priya continued their journey, the memory of their encounter with the rickshaw puller lingered, serving as a poignant reminder of the enduring power of kindness and perspective in shaping our lives.

XI

Celebration

On a Sunday afternoon, as dark clouds loomed overhead and thunder rumbled in the distance, Rohit hurriedly prepared for his theatre class amidst the onset of rain. His father's reminder to close the door behind him echoed in the background, countered by his mother's insistence on attending to it herself due to the inclement weather.

Amidst this familial exchange, Rohit couldn't help but reflect on the significance of Mother's Day. To him, it wasn't merely a once-a-year occasion for social media posts, but a continuous celebration that unfolded every day in the countless tasks and sacrifices his mother made.

As Rohit embarked on his journey, he carried with him a profound appreciation for his mother's unwavering dedication and selflessness, recognizing that her love and care transcended any single day of recognition.

Through this simple exchange, the enduring bond between mother and child shines, emphasizing the timeless nature of maternal love and the everyday heroism found in the ordinary moments of family life.

This reflection serves as a poignant reminder of the immeasurable value of maternal love and the importance of expressing gratitude for it not just on designated holidays, but every day of the year.

XII
Realization

Mr. Chatterjee's life had been marked by profound loss and unexpected challenges. Following the passing of his first wife, Lily, due to tuberculosis, he found solace in the companionship of Sarala, who stepped into Lily's shoes with unwavering dedication. However, despite Sarala's efforts to nurture their family, she could never replace the bond between Mr. Chatterjee's son, Prasenjit, and his biological mother.

As Prasenjit grew into adolescence, his actions became increasingly reckless, unchecked by the absence of disciplinary guidance. Tragically, one fateful day, Prasenjit's daredevil behavior led to a devastating accident at a traffic signal, leaving him gravely injured and fighting for his life.

Mr. Chatterjee rushed to his son's side, only to receive the heart-wrenching news that Prasenjit's kidneys had ceased to function. Desperate to save his son, Mr. Chatterjee embarked on a frantic search for a kidney donor, leaving no stone unturned in his quest to find a match.

After exhausting every avenue, Mr. Chatterjee's prayers were answered when a donor's kidney was miraculously secured, paving the way for Prasenjit's recovery. In a poignant moment of gratitude and reconciliation, Prasenjit, overcome with emotion, uttered a single word that echoed with decades of longing and forgiveness:

"Maa!"

This powerful moment served as a testament to the enduring bond between stepmother and stepson, transcending years of misunderstanding and resentment. It underscored the capacity for love and redemption, even in the face of life's most harrowing trials.

A gentle reminder of the transformative power of love, forgiveness, and the enduring strength of the human spirit.

Snapshots of Everyday Moments

XIII

Umbrella

Amidst the relentless downpour, Anjali found herself navigating the soaked streets, her oversight of forgetting her umbrella compounded by the heavy rain. However, amidst the deluge, a simple act of kindness unfolded before her eyes.

An elderly gentleman, Rajesh, crossed paths with Anjali, offering her his umbrella in a gesture of selflessness. Though their shared shelter left them both equally soaked by the rain, the warmth of human connection outweighed the discomfort of wet clothes.

Grateful for Rajesh's kindness, Anjali engaged in a brief exchange of gratitude. It was then that she learned of Rajesh's humble occupation as a laborer in the construction sector, his resilience mirrored in his willingness to offer assistance despite his circumstances.

Moved by Rajesh's words, Anjali was reminded of the innate goodness that resides within humanity. In the face of adversity and scarcity, Rajesh's act of generosity exemplified the true spirit of compassion and empathy.

Through this encounter, Anjali gained a deeper appreciation for the boundless capacity for kindness that exists within each of us, regardless of our station in life. Amidst life's storms, it is these acts of selflessness that serve as beacons of hope, illuminating the path toward a more compassionate and caring world.

XIV
Window Seat

Aditya's preference for the window seat during childhood was a steadfast tradition, a cherished privilege that brought him joy and excitement during family travels. However, since tying the knot with his beloved Suhaani, Aditya's priorities have shifted, and with it, his selflessness has blossomed.

In a beautiful display of love and consideration, Aditya willingly sacrifices the coveted window seat for Suhaani's comfort and happiness. As they embark on journeys together, Aditya finds fulfillment not in claiming the window seat for himself, but in witnessing Suhaani's joy and contentment by his side.

Throughout their five-year marriage, Aditya has consistently placed Suhaani's needs and preferences above his own, embracing the role of a devoted partner with grace and tenderness. Yet, amidst this selfless act of love, Aditya is left pondering three profound questions.

Is he merely a child yearning for his desires?

Or has he matured into a selfless and caring husband, prioritizing his partner's happiness above all else?

Is his gesture of relinquishing the window seat an act of love, a testament to the depth of his devotion, or is it simply a compromise, a concession made for the sake of marital harmony?

As Aditya grapples with these questions, he realizes that the true essence of their journey lies not in the answers themselves but in the shared experiences, laughter, and love they continue to cultivate together. In the end, the tale of Aditya's selfless sacrifice captures the profound beauty of love, highlighting the transformative power of putting the needs of others before our own.

XV
Circle

Rohit found himself unexpectedly summoned to serve as an interviewer for a job opening—an opportunity that signified the fulfillment of a vow he had made to himself within the first five years of his career: to sit on the opposite side of the table.

As he prepared to evaluate candidates for the same role he once pursued, Rohit couldn't help but reflect on the journey that had brought him here. Rejected in the past, he now sat in a position to assess and select candidates, some of whom may have previously turned him away.

This experience transcended mere professional advancement; it was a moment of personal triumph—a testament to Rohit's growth and resilience. Each candidate he interviewed offered a chance to reconcile with his past, reaffirm his value, and demonstrate the extent of his progress.

In this cyclical nature of life, Rohit discovered not only an opportunity to settle scores with his past but also to embrace the richness of his journey. With each interview, he found solace in the understanding that setbacks and rejections are not endpoints but rather stepping stones toward success.

Yet, amidst the interviews, Rohit grappled with internal conflicts and moments of realization. Interactions with candidates served as poignant reminders of his own experiences, fostering a deeper sense of empathy and understanding.

Ultimately, Rohit's experience as an interviewer was not solely about filling a job opening; it was about navigating the complexities of life, finding strength in adversity, and seizing every opportunity for growth and self-discovery.

As he made his selections and concluded the interviews, Rohit did so with a profound sense of gratitude for the transformative journey that had led him to this moment—a moment that encapsulated the essence of resilience, redemption, and the enduring pursuit of personal fulfillment.

XVI
Night Bus

As the clock neared 8:30 P.M., Rajeev made his way home from the office, the city enveloped in the soft glow of evening lights. A bus glided to a stop before him, and a familiar figure disembarked, waving enthusiastically.

It was the bus conductor, someone Rajeev recognized but whose name escaped him.

"Remember me, Sir? I'm Bappa," the man exclaimed. "I've noticed you haven't been on our bus lately. Is everything alright, Sir?"

Rajeev nodded, offering a small smile. "Ah, yes, my office location has changed. That's why you haven't seen me around. How have you been, Bappa?"

Bappa's expression softened into a sad tone. "I'm managing, Sir. Trying my hand at becoming a driver now."

"I see," Rajeev replied, noting the absence of Bappa's usual rush to catch stragglers. "You always did have a knack for keeping things lively on the bus, even if it meant running a bit late."

With a touch of advice in his voice, Rajeev added, "Take care, Bappa. Don't rush too much. Leaving a few minutes earlier can make all the difference."

Bappa's face lit up with a suggestion. "Driver, let's drop Sir home. It's been a while since we've had a chance to chat."

As they embarked on the journey home, Rajeev reflected silently, realizing that amidst the complexities of life—be it fluctuating job roles, uncertain relationships, or professional setbacks—simple acts of kindness and connection could uplift the spirits.

After a taxing day at the office, filled with challenges and setbacks, this unexpected encounter left Rajeev feeling buoyed by human warmth and camaraderie.

As they reached his stop, Rajeev turned to Bappa with a grateful smile, conveying more than words ever could—thank you for brightening his evening.

XVII
After 6 years

On a tranquil Sunday morning, the ancestral Roy Villa in Kolkata hosted a crucial meeting. The gathering's purpose? To deliberate on the future of this cherished family abode, now teetering on the brink of neglect as its custodian, Purab, the youngest of six brothers at 60, found himself shouldering its upkeep alone. His son engrossed in the pursuits of NGO work and scholarly endeavors, seemed disconnected from familial responsibility.

Amidst the discussions, a proposition emerged from a real estate developer, offering an enticing package of monetary compensation and apartments. Some siblings, recognizing the impracticality of maintaining their portions, leaned towards selling. Yet, the prospect of strangers inhabiting a house steeped in familial history weighed heavy on their hearts.

Enter the next generation, whose impassioned plea for preservation breathed new life into the debate. Firm in their resolve, they rejected the notion of demolition, choosing instead to uphold the legacy of their childhood sanctuary. Pooling resources, they initiated a voluntary fund to sustain the home's maintenance.

Six years have since passed, and the Roy Villa resonates once more with laughter, love, and cherished memories. Every festive season, the Roy family congregates, reaffirming their commitment to the enduring spirit of kinship and tradition that defines their lineage.

XVIII

Hum 7 -7 hain

A prestigious Inter School Science Exhibition was scheduled to grace the halls of Delhi Public School, Kolkata. Among the participants, Jayanta, Pamela, and Shubhabrata formed a team with a mission to illuminate the intricacies of acids and bases through the lens of litmus and pH testing.

In meticulous preparation leading up to the event, every detail was carefully orchestrated, each element poised for presentation.

However, on the fateful day of the exhibition, dismay greeted the trio as they discovered their samples had vanished without a trace. With time ticking away and their contingency plans exhausted, despair threatened to overshadow their aspirations.

Yet, in the face of adversity, Jayanta emerged as the beacon of resilience and resourcefulness. Venturing into the school's canteen and medical room, he ingeniously procured substitutes, transforming everyday items into potent symbols of scientific inquiry.

With renewed confidence, the team reassembled, their resolve unwavering despite earlier doubts. Through Jayanta's eloquence and unwavering determination, the demonstration unfolded with seamless grace, captivating the audience and earning accolades.

Their triumph, securing the second prize, was a testament to the power of teamwork and unwavering belief in oneself. When pressed by TTIS on their remarkable feat, Jayanta humbly attributed their success to collective effort, acknowledging the indispensable role each member played in the journey. Shubhabrata, while acknowledging Jayanta's pivotal role, emphasized the unity and perseverance that propelled them forward, echoing the sentiment that "together, we achieved greatness."

In the end, it was not just a victory in the exhibition but a testament to the indomitable spirit and camaraderie that defines true teamwork.

XIX

8 P.M. Call

At 8 P.M. IST, tension filled the air. The Client Partner vented frustration towards the India-based MNC's IT team during the Weekly Status call. The cause? A significant production failure that had severely impacted business operations.

In response, a high-level meeting was convened, gathering Senior Managers and Directors to dissect the root cause of the failure. The lead of the project responsible for the problematic product found themselves under intense scrutiny.

In a pivotal moment, Sunil, the Project Manager, stepped forward, shouldering the responsibility. With unwavering conviction, he declared, "The fault lies with me. Neither my team nor my lead, Saurabh, should bear the blame." Without hesitation, he appealed directly to the Client Manager, pleading for a solitary opportunity to rectify the situation.

The Client Manager granted a six-month ultimatum for a solution to be implemented. Sunil rallied Saurabh, urging him to give his all to the task at hand.

Six months later, during another late-night call, Sunil was lauded for overseeing a flawless delivery, achieved within stringent budget constraints. The client team expressed their satisfaction with the outcome.

In a selfless gesture, Sunil arranged for Saurabh to lead a meeting with senior management, showcasing his adept handling of the project, from inception to seamless delivery. Amidst accolades and applause, Saurabh took the stage.

Reflecting on the journey, he acknowledged Sunil's exemplary leadership, stating, "This success is owed to my manager, Sunil, who courageously accepted blame in times of adversity and propelled me into the spotlight of success. True leadership entails owning failures and sharing successes."

In closing, Saurabh expressed gratitude for the invaluable lesson learned during the fateful 8 P.M. call, vowing to embody such leadership qualities in his endeavors.

XX

Colors

In the quiet hours of the night, Rohit and Meera engaged in a heartfelt conversation about their shared aspirations for the future. Their journey had begun through a matrimonial site, and navigating the initial awkwardness of meeting as strangers had been a challenge they courageously embraced.

Over six months, their bond deepened, evolving from mere acquaintances to devoted partners. Yet, amidst the seemingly smooth sailing, Rohit unexpectedly broached the topic of separation. Meera, unfazed, responded with grace, accepting the decision with mutual understanding.

In a poignant moment, Meera expressed her anticipation for the new chapter ahead, humorously dubbing Rohit as "Mr. Husband," signaling their imminent transition from boyfriend-girlfriend to spouses. Their registry marriage, scheduled for the following day, promised to mark the official commencement of their shared journey.

Among the many quirks they shared, their mutual aversion to Holi colors stood out. However, as the eve of the festival unfolded, Rohit broke tradition by applying a symbolic red hue to Meera's forehead. In this tender exchange, the couple defied their usual reluctance towards colors, embracing the moment with unbridled joy and mutual affection.

As they reveled in the spirit of the occasion, Rohit and Meera found solace in each other's company, cherishing the start of their new life together.

XXI

Waves

"Where is the sailor?" cried the middle-aged woman as she scanned the expanse of Golden Beach in Odisha.

The family had set out for an early morning stroll along the shore, their attention drawn to a lone fisherman navigating his boat into the tumultuous waters of the Bay of Bengal.

The relentless, erratic waves posed a formidable challenge, with the sailor valiantly battling to maintain control of his vessel. Suddenly, to the horror of onlookers, the boat capsized, disappearing beneath the waves, leaving only a tangle of blue fishing nets in its wake.

Perplexed murmurs rippled through the gathered crowd as they watched the unfolding drama. Then, as if out of nowhere, a turtle appeared, ensnared in the wreckage near the boat's radar.

Amidst the chaos, the sailor emerged, grappling with both the boat and the unexpected sea creature. After a fierce struggle, they managed to free themselves, but not before the turtle's injured form was revealed, destined to be washed ashore by the relentless waves.

With a solemn gaze, the turtle seemed to convey its gratitude to the sailor, who, in a moment of empathy, propelled the creature back into the safety of the sea, despite his struggles.

In that silent exchange, the sailor understood the profound interconnectedness of life at sea. Each, in their way, depended on the ocean for survival – one to harvest its bounty, the other to inhabit its depths.

As they rode the waves toward their respective destinies, the beauty and danger of the sea were laid bare. And while the shore may bask in its tranquil beauty, it is the relentless rhythm of the waves that shape the true essence of the sea.

XXII

Kolkata Café

On a damp, rainy day, a solitary figure parked their bike near a quaint café. Hurriedly approaching the counter, he overheard a shrill voice placing an order, "One Darjeeling Tea with two spoons of sugar."

Taking inspiration, he quirkily chimed in, "One Darjeeling Tea with Raindrops only, no sugar."

Startled, the girl behind the counter exclaimed, "Raindrops? Are you sure?"

At that moment, she recognized him as a classmate, one who had always observed her silently but never uttered a word.

Reflecting on this unexpected encounter, the girl retreated to a secluded corner table by the window.

Unable to find another seat, the boy joined her, prompting a smile from the girl.

Teasingly, she remarked, "Your rainy Darjeeling Tea antics. Have you ever tried it before? A girl isn't won over by tea alone; you need to speak too."

With a hint of bashfulness, the boy responded, "I can speak, but in your presence, words seem to elude me... and no, I've never tasted this kind of tea before."

Curiously, the girl inquired, "Then why today?"

His reply was simple yet sincere, "Because today I saw you, and I wanted your company."

Before the girl could respond, he ordered, "Two Kolkata Cafe Darjeeling Teas, one with sugar and the other with raindrops."

With a playful grin, he countered, "With such sweet company, who needs sugar?"

Bantering back, she teased, "So, you're saying you'll never need sugar when I'm around? The sugar mills will go bankrupt."

Confidently, he declared, "Well, I'll certainly be in profit then. How about this time tomorrow, Kolkata Cafe?"

Her response was lighthearted, "Only if it rains!"

As laughter filled the room, mingling with the soothing sound of raindrops, Kolkata Cafe became a sanctuary of warmth and connection.

XXIII
DSLR

Rohit's father handed him a new DSLR camera, eager to pass on the torch of photography. "This is your new DSLR camera. How do you click?" he asked, hoping for guidance.

Lost in his phone, Rohit barely registered his father's inquiry. Seeing no response, the ex-bank manager began to leave the room, feeling hesitant to intrude.

Suddenly, Rohit snapped out of his distraction and exclaimed, "Dad! This one's for you! No more Kodak KB10. This DSLR is yours from now on."

Surprised but touched by his son's gesture, his father smiled, "I'm content with my old camera. I'm too old for these modern gadgets."

"Sorry, Dad, but this is for you," Rohit insisted. "I remember how you patiently captured moments, holding back emotions to get the perfect shot. Consider this DSLR a tribute to your photography. Don't worry, the KB10 will still be around, but this will be your new toy."

With Rohit's encouragement, his father tentatively explored the features of the DSLR, learning a few techniques along the way.

His first subject was his wife, adorned in a vibrant red saree, captured within a wooden frame. With a tearful yet proud smile, he spoke to her image, "This is a DSLR. Its full form? 'Duty Should be Love and Respect.' I love you! You look amazing, like a queen!"

In that moment, he paid homage not only to his wife but to all the creators of cherished memories. To both seasoned veterans and novice enthusiasts, he offered his heartfelt appreciation.

• 49 •

Unveiling Self

XXIV
Independence

At approximately 0200 hours, yet another violation of the ceasefire occurred in the Poonch sector.

Subedar Ratan Singh swiftly issued orders, directing the armed forces to respond firmly to the provocations.

In the darkness of the night, enemy personnel attempted to breach our country's border.

During the skirmish, a bullet fired by our troops critically injured one of the infiltrators.

In his final moments, the wounded soldier, identified as Md Imran, pleaded for water from our army generals.

Responding to his plea, Subedar Singh offered a compassionate gesture, providing the much-needed water. Moments later, Md Imran succumbed to his injuries.

His last words echoed with poignancy, "Thank you for the humanity shown. We are all human beings serving our nations. I wish we were not divided by partition; then we could have been brothers."

"Desh toh sabka apna apna ho gaya, par log paraya ho gaya..."

XXV

Rich

Tiya, a sweet young girl in her third year of college, embarked on a Durga Pujo shopping excursion to Esplanade. On her way back, she indulged in an ice cream to soothe her parched throat.

Amidst the hustle and bustle of the crowded pavement, she noticed a man selling handkerchiefs, accompanied by his daughter. Nearby, a lady emerged from a luxury car, seemingly interested in purchasing a handkerchief. However, after meticulously inspecting each item and deeming them unsatisfactory, she departed without making a purchase.

Observing the disappointment on the faces of the seller and his daughter, Tiya felt compelled to act. Despite not needing any handkerchiefs herself, she approached the stall and purchased three without hesitation or negotiation.

This simple act of kindness illuminated the faces of the father and daughter, transforming their gloom into gratitude. Tiya understood that true wealth lies not in material possessions but in the richness of the heart. Her actions exemplified the essence of humanity – the ability to bring joy and comfort to others, even in small gestures.

As the adage goes, "We are rich by heart, not by the wealth or luxuries we possess." Tiya's gesture serves as a poignant reminder of the power of compassion to uplift and inspire, transcending barriers of wealth or status.

XXVI

Dreams

Two vehicles, an office bus , and a school bus, found themselves parked side by side at a bustling road intersection, patiently waiting for the traffic signal to change.

In that momentary pause, each bus cast a glance at the other, silently acknowledging their respective aspirations and enviable attributes.

XXVII

Trust

A father and his young daughter were crossing a bridge together. Sensing her father's unease, the little girl offered to hold his hand for safety.

"Sweetheart, please hold my hand so that you don't fall into the river," the father requested.

To his surprise, the little girl replied, "No, Dad. You hold my hand."

Puzzled, the father asked, "What's the difference?"

With wisdom beyond her years, the little girl explained, "There's a big difference. If I hold your hand and something happens to me, I may accidentally let go. But if you hold my hand, I know that no matter what happens, you will never let me go."

In this simple exchange lies a profound truth: trust is not merely about physical grasp, but about the unbreakable bond between hearts. It's about knowing that, in times of uncertainty, the one you love will always stand by your side, unwavering and steadfast.

So, let us remember to cherish and nurture the bonds of trust in our relationships. Let us choose to hold the hand of our loved ones with unwavering commitment and love, leaving the rest unsaid.

In the end, it is the strength of our bonds that truly sustains us through life's journey.

XXVIII

God

In the early hours of the morning, a line had formed at an ATM, with people eagerly waiting to withdraw money. Among them stood a young man in his mid-twenties and an elderly pensioner.

As hours passed, the strain of standing took its toll on the pensioner, who suddenly fell ill. With no medical assistance in sight, the young man sprang into action. He escorted the elderly gentleman to a nearby clinic, ensuring he received the care he needed, and then accompanied him back to his home. Generously, he even provided the pensioner with some Rs. 100 notes to ease his expenses in the coming days.

Grateful beyond words, the elderly man expressed his heartfelt appreciation, reflecting on the kindness shown to him. He lamented the absence of his own family to witness such compassionate gestures, musing that those who extend help to strangers are likely to care for their parents as if they were divine.

With a humble smile, the young man, orphaned and without familial ties, pondered the notion, "Perhaps in another life..."

Ultimately, when they finally reached the ATM to withdraw money, something unexpected occurred. Instead of debiting their accounts, both individuals found that their accounts had been credited with something far more valuable than money: humanity.

In a world often tainted by greed and corruption, this simple act of compassion served as a reminder of the inherent goodness within humanity, transcending the boundaries of wealth and status.

The unforeseen consequence of #BanBlackMoney was the emergence of a precious gift to humanity—a renewed sense of compassion and goodwill.

XXIX

Respect

The cheap but glaring, colorful light bulbs cast a superficial shine on Aman's face as he stood amidst the best-rated brothel in Kolkata, negotiating over a suitable companion for the night. After the initial transaction was completed, he was handed his 'order' and led to a room adorned with gaudy decorations and lewd pictures. As the door closed behind them, the girl mechanically inquired, "Would you like me to undress myself, or would you prefer to do it yourself?"

Meeting her gaze head-on, Aman responded, "Neither, darling. I'm not here to consume your femininity. Put on your jacket. We're going to catch a movie. The show starts in 30 minutes. Hurry!"

The girl stood there, mouth agape, unsure of how to react. Aman offered her a reassuring smile and gestured for her to follow his lead.

Together, they left the room to watch a film at a nearby theater. Afterward, they dined together at a posh restaurant in the city.

As Aman accompanied her back to her place, the woman spoke up, "I'm not sure what your intentions are, but I'm deeply grateful to you for treating me like a human being for the first time in my life. Thank you for your kindness."

Aman replied calmly, "Don't mistake this for any emotion like love. I simply wanted a companion to share the night with, to savor the joys of life, and to create lasting memories. You fulfilled that role. I respect you as a person, and that's how I've treated you. That's the extent of it, sweetheart. Good night."

With that, Aman turned and walked away, disappearing into the mist. The woman watched him until he was out of sight before heading back home, her mind buzzing with a whirlwind of colorful emotions and memories.

XXX

Unaccomplished

A lady reporter approached the budding writer with a probing question, "Have you ever experienced profound love that remains untold in your stories?"

The writer, taken aback, countered, "What leads you to such an assumption, Madam?"

The reporter elaborated, "Your writings often revolve around unfulfilled love, garnering attention from readers."

With a dismissive smile, the writer responded, "We needn't live a hundred lives to craft a hundred stories. These narratives stem from our imagination, breathing life into our characters."

Undeterred, the reporter pressed on, "So, there hasn't been any real-life inspiration?"

The writer affirmed, "Not at all. These are merely creative musings unrelated to my personal experiences."

The discussion continued for another three minutes until it was time for the writer's conclusion. As the audience watched, the lady reporter and the writer exchanged handshakes. Little did they know the inner turmoil beneath the surface—how difficult it was for the lady to conceal her tears, and how agonizing it was for the writer to mask a blatant lie. Unbeknownst to all, the duo shared a poignant history, an unofficial union that ended in a courtroom three years prior, marked by two signatures that sealed the fate of their unfulfilled love.

Traditional lineage & Celebrations

XXXI

Mahalaya or Pitri-Pokho?

Amit's tradition of visiting the Baghbazar Ganga ghat with his father, Dibakar, during Durga Pujo each year was a cherished ritual, marking the conclusion of the festivities with the immersion of idols on Dashami eve.

Now, on the early morning of Mahalaya, Amit finds himself at the same ghat, but for a different purpose. Alone, he performs "Tarpan" for his deceased father, a solemn duty he undertakes annually.

As he recites the Sanskrit slokas under the guidance of the priest, Amit feels a profound connection to his father. In his mind's eye, he sees himself holding his father's hand, just as they used to wander the ghats together.

Though the mode of communication has shifted, the bond between them remains unbroken. While others may view the transition from Pitri Pokho to Devi Pokkho, for Amit, the spirit of Pitripokho endures indefinitely.

XXXII
Dwitiya Pakkha

It had been nearly three years since Avik and Malini finalized their divorce in the Kolkata High Court. Avik had to part with a substantial alimony to sever ties with her.

Word had spread among their common friends that Malini had swiftly married Avik's boss the very next year. Avik couldn't help but reminisce about the eight years he had invested in their relationship before their marriage, only to see it all crumble. Their three-year-old daughter, Prerana, remained with Avik, as Malini had opted to sever all ties with him.

Pressured by Avik's parents, he eventually decided to embark on a second marriage, tying the knot with a woman named Ajanta. Remarkably, Ajanta embraced Prerana as her own, showering her with love and care that rivaled that of a biological mother, if not surpassing it at times.

In due time, Avik and Ajanta welcomed a son into their lives, and they found joy in their new abode in New Town. Reflecting on nearly a decade of their union, Avik realized that he had achieved everything he had ever dreamed of. The pinnacle of happiness for him was witnessing the birth of their son, a moment he never thought possible after his divorce.

Curious about Ajanta's perspective, Avik queried how she managed to navigate their complex familial dynamics. Ajanta's response was both profound and heartfelt, "While you may see this as your second chance, I view it as our only chance to find happiness together. More importantly, I love you. Your concerns about Prerana are unwarranted—she carries your genes, and that's all that matters to me. Now, please excuse me, I need to prepare Prerana for her dance function."

Indeed, the concept of a second marriage, symbolized by Dwitiya, can bring unexpected joy and fulfillment, proving that sometimes, a fresh start can lead to beautiful outcomes.

XXXIII

Tritiyo

Sumi, a transgender woman residing in the slums of Kalighat, identified herself as a girl despite the challenges she faced.

As an orphan without anyone to support her, Sumi endured hardship to complete her Class 12 exams. She relied on tuition to cover her school fees, facing ridicule from classmates along the way.

Undeterred, Sumi pursued higher education, enrolling in college to pursue a Bachelor's degree in English. Consciously avoiding Science due to its higher tuition and lab fees, she forged ahead with her chosen path.

Upon graduating with honors in English, Sumi pursued a Master's degree in the same subject. In her spare time, she diligently worked on writing a book.

Despite never seeking publication, Sumi's teacher, Mrs. Halder, discovered her manuscript and was impressed by its quality. With Mrs. Halder's encouragement, Sumi approached a renowned publication house, only to face rejection upon revealing her identity.

Undeterred by setbacks, Sumi persevered, eventually finding a local publishing house willing to take a chance on her book, "His/Her Train of Dreams."

The book became a sensation, garnering widespread acclaim and even earning Sumi the prestigious Booker Prize Award in 2015, surpassing renowned authors worldwide.

During the press conference, when asked whom she would dedicate her award to, Sumi acknowledged Mrs. Halder's support but emphasized that her success was her own. She expressed gratitude for the adversity she faced, which fueled her determination to succeed.

Asked about thanking God, Sumi declined, asserting that she had completed herself and owed her success solely to her efforts.

The Prime Minister congratulated Sumi, recognizing her as a source of pride for India and challenging societal norms surrounding gender identity.

Sumi's journey serves as a testament to resilience, determination, and self-empowerment, transcending societal expectations and inspiring others to embrace their true selves.

XXXIV

Nabami

Siddharth, a B.Tech student at Jadavpur University, found solace in the company of books, his closest companions.

His world shifted when he stumbled upon a vivacious girl dancing exuberantly in the canteen to a Bollywood tune.

Mesmerized, Siddharth could only watch in awe, lacking the courage to inquire about her.

Their paths crossed again in the central library on an early Monday morning, where the girl introduced herself as Nabami and questioned Siddharth's perpetual bookish solitude.

Prompted by Nabami's invitation, Siddharth ventured beyond his literary realm, embracing the gift of friendship she offered.

As Pujo holidays approached, they bid temporary farewell, with Nabami residing outside Kolkata.

Yet, Siddharth vowed to cherish Pujo, carrying Nabami's spirit with him throughout the festivities.

Eager to express his feelings, Siddharth planned to meet Nabami on Durga Pujo's Nabami, obtaining her address from a friend.

Arriving at Nabami's home, Siddharth was met with resistance from her mother, unaware of Nabami's condition.

Upon seeing Nabami, now battling cancer and adorned with a scarf, Siddharth poured out his heart, professing his love and pledging to fight alongside her.

In a moment of shared vulnerability, Nabami reciprocated Siddharth's affection, acknowledging their shared journey and the bond they forged.

Their fate remains uncertain, but in each other's company, they find solace and happiness amidst life's trials.

This poignant tale reminds us of the enduring power of love and companionship, even in the face of adversity.

XXXV

Shubho Dashami

Riya, a school student, eagerly anticipates Durga Puja like many others.

As Dashami, the final day of Pujo, arrives, she experiences a pang of sadness as the festivities come to a close.

Turning to her mother, Riya questions why Durga Puja occurs only once a year, expressing a desire for its more frequent occurrence.

In response, Riya's mother offers a wise perspective, explaining that the joy of Durga Puja is heightened by its rarity. She emphasizes the significance of anticipation, noting that the excitement and anticipation build over the year, culminating in the exhilaration of Pujo's arrival.

Acknowledging Riya's disappointment, her mother encourages her to cherish the memories of this year's Puja and eagerly await the next. She reminds Riya that good things often come with patience and anticipation, enhancing the enjoyment of the experience.

Riya's mother also suggests finding joy in other celebrations throughout the year and indulging in traditional sweets, like rosogolla, to mark the auspicious occasion of Bijoya Dashami.

Ending on a heartfelt note, Riya's mother imparts her blessings, invoking the spirit of victory over adversity symbolized by Durga's triumph over the demon Asura.

In this exchange, Riya learns the value of patience, anticipation, and savoring the special moments that come only once in a while.

XXXVI
Chaar

Anil was employed by the central government, working diligently at the Reserve Bank of India in Mumbai.

His union with Maya was the product of an arranged marriage, facilitated by a distant relative.

Two years into their marital journey, Anil and Maya resolved to extend their family.

Remarkably, Anil harbored no preference regarding the gender of their child; to him, a son or daughter held equal significance.

Yet, secretly, he nurtured a desire for a son, aspiring to perpetuate his lineage.

Upon the arrival of their firstborn, a daughter, lovingly named Krishna by Maya, Anil concealed his yearning for a son, sharing it with none.

Over the following five years, Maya endured the trials of childbirth thrice more, each time welcoming a daughter into their lives: Kaveri, Ganga, and Yamuna.

The strain of multiple pregnancies left Maya weakened, and her health compromised.

Anil's mother, voicing her hopes for a grandson to carry on the family name, added to the unspoken pressure.

Reluctantly relinquishing his dream of a son, Anil resolved to provide his daughters with the finest education and opportunities.

His daughters flourished, all four emerging as accomplished software engineers.

Today, happily married and residing in Mumbai, the daughters remain steadfastly devoted to their parents, eschewing opportunities elsewhere to ensure their continued presence and care.

Their husbands, embracing their roles as integral members of the family, foster an environment where the distinction between 'son' and 'son-in-law' is blurred.

Meanwhile, Anil's brother, Sunil, blessed with a son who has since settled in the United States, finds himself and his ailing wife consigned to the solitude of an old-age home.

For Anil, Maya, and their cherished 'sons' and daughters, fortnightly Sundays are cherished moments of togetherness, imbued with profound meaning.

Reflecting on his initial desire for a son, Anil realizes that in his four daughters, he has gained not just daughters, but sons too.

In the end, the arrival of four 'Betis' has brought four more 'Betas' into their lives, enriching their family in ways they could never have imagined.

To Anil and Maya, every child, regardless of gender, is their 'Beta'.

XXXVII
Pujo Days

The seemingly perfect couple parted ways just before Pujo, a festival dear to their hearts.

For five years, Saahil and Leena had embraced Pujo as a time for hand-in-hand strolls through the vibrant streets of Kolkata, adorned in their finest attire. Among their cherished ensembles was a Sherwani gifted by Leena and a saree bestowed by Saahil.

This year, however, Saahil found himself devoid of plans, lacking the motivation to even contemplate making any. He ventured out only once, reluctantly meeting with his college friends.

Meanwhile, Leena immersed herself in the festivities, joining her friends for pandal hopping from Dwitiya onwards, seeking solace or perhaps distraction amidst the Pujo fervor.

The dynamics shifted within a matter of days or months.

Previously, Saahil would vehemently oppose any plans his father made to venture outside Kolkata during Pujo, staunchly advocating for the sanctity of celebrating the festival within the city's bounds. Yet now, he harbored a desire to escape, longing to leave behind what he once deemed the "best place on earth."

Conversely, Leena once enamored with the hustle and bustle of Pujo crowds, now preferred the tranquility of home during the festive days, seeking solace in solitude.

Two individuals, once united by their shared affection for Pujo, now find themselves separated by the complexities of love and divergent emotions.

XXXVIII
Diwali Celebration

The clock struck 8 A.M. on Diwali morning, and Sujata found herself immersed in preparations, arranging crackers and diyas with meticulous care.

The atmosphere buzzed with anticipation as the residents of "Retirement House" in Benaras geared up to celebrate Diwali in grand style.

Assisting Sujata in her endeavors were Amit and, later, Sadhana, adding to the collective sense of excitement.

A specially curated menu awaited the evening festivities, featuring delectable Fried Rice and Kashmiri Alur Dam, promising a feast to remember.

As dusk descended, the air filled with the scent of sweets and the crackle of fireworks, enveloping everyone in joyous celebration.

Amidst the backdrop of "Retirement House," it became evident that the spirits of its residents were far from retired, their zest for life shines through in every moment of happiness shared.

Let us uphold this spirit of liveliness, embracing happiness as our guiding principle , and celebrate Diwali.

May the "IF" block of life, with happiness as its statement, continue to execute indefinitely, never veering into the "ELSE" loop of sadness.

XXXIX

Happy Anniversary

It was December 9th, 2023, marking Abdul and Fatima's first year of marriage.

Abdul, a hardworking laborer, toiled each day, saving every penny to surprise his beloved wife on their anniversary.

With great determination, Abdul had managed to set aside Rs. 800, a modest sum, to purchase a gift for his cherished "home minister."

On the eve of December 8th, Abdul embarked on a quest to find the perfect saree, aspiring to gift Fatima a Banarasi masterpiece. However, his aspirations were met with disappointment as the finest saree shops in Kolkata were beyond his budgetary reach.

Resigned to his financial constraints, Abdul settled for a replica Banarasi saree from a more affordable store, though his heart yearned for the genuine article.

Upon his return home, Abdul eagerly awaited the stroke of midnight, anticipating the exchange of gifts.

To his surprise, Fatima roused him from his slumber, presenting him with a gift wrapped in colorful paper. With bated breath, Abdul unwrapped the package to find a stylish T-shirt nestled within.

In a heartwarming gesture, Fatima also unveiled the saree that Abdul had purchased, her eyes gleaming with delight as she declared it her very first Banarasi saree.

Despite Abdul's admission that the saree was not authentic, Fatima's response was one of unwavering gratitude and affection, cherishing the gift from her beloved husband.

Their anniversary celebration continued with a simple yet meaningful meal of Khichuri, shared from a single plate as a symbol of their unity and mutual support.

Tears of joy welled in Abdul's eyes as he realized the depth of love and contentment he shared with Fatima, transcending material possessions and worldly desires.

Though they lacked the means to host extravagant parties or exchange lavish gifts, the bond between Abdul and Fatima was imbued with genuine, unadulterated love.

In the end, it wasn't the authenticity of the saree that mattered, but the authenticity of their love—a love that remained pure and steadfast, despite life's hardships and limitations.

XL

Rohan- Priyanshi's New Year

Rohan, an official Sony TV mechanic, is accustomed to receiving calls from customers seeking assistance with their television sets. On the early morning of New Year's Day, he receives an urgent call from Priyanshi, who resides in a distant area of Howrah, requesting a prompt fix for her Tata Sky connection, as she has an important event to watch.

Without hesitation, Rohan swiftly mobilizes, departing for Priyanshi's location within just 30 minutes, accompanied by his driver. Throughout the journey, Priyanshi's calls persistently punctuate the air, inquiring about Rohan's progress.

However, Rohan encounters an unexpected delay as he gets caught up at a railway signal crossing. Despite the setback, he reassures Priyanshi of his imminent arrival.

Upon reaching Priyanshi's residence, Rohan is greeted by an unexpected sight. Priyanshi, a specially-abled woman with no sight, awaits his assistance.

Undeterred by the challenge, Rohan diligently sets to work, swiftly fixing the TV connection. With a smile, he announces to Priyanshi, "Madam, your TV is now fixed."

To Rohan's surprise, Priyanshi's reaction is not one of solitary gratitude. Instead, her proclamation fills the room with the lively chatter of numerous children from various age groups.

They have gathered eagerly to watch the grand finale of "Sa Re Ga Ma Little Champs."

Puzzled, Rohan queries Priyanshi about her enjoyment of the television program despite her visual impairment.

Priyanshi responds with profound wisdom, explaining that she experiences the joy of television through the expressive descriptions of the children around her. For her, the true value lies in the shared experience and sense of togetherness.

Filled with a sense of fulfillment, Rohan realizes the significance of his work, especially on the auspicious first day of the new year.

In that moment, he understands that his role extends beyond mere technical repairs; it serves as a conduit for bringing people together and fostering moments of shared happiness.

XLI

Bangla New Year - Shubho Noboborsho

"Start the taxi," Avira commanded the owner sharply, her voice laced with urgency, "and keep following the black Honda City." Without hesitation, the taxi owner complied, swiftly initiating the meter as instructed. Avira stepped into the City Bar, her destination now in sight: the parked black sedan. Avira found herself thrust into countless unforeseen situations, all of which had been concealed from her by Malik. "You belong to me," Malik often reminded her, "and your actions should reverberate across the country for maximum impact." Security was a foreign concept within her realm of existence, according to Malik's teachings. "You are a woman desired by many," Malik would preach, emphasizing her allure as a tool of influence. Avira had spent countless days and nights in the company of strangers, obediently carrying out Malik's orders. At times, she feared for her life, but miraculously, she always emerged unscathed. "You are not here to perish but to serve," Malik would remind her, instilling a sense of purpose amidst the chaos. Her family was provided for with generous monthly deposits into their bank account, courtesy of Malik. Despite once harboring dreams of marrying her childhood crush, Avira had resigned herself to this life, her only prayer being for her family's safety, even if it meant sacrificing her own. Today, Malik had tasked her with trailing the black sedan. Inside the bar, she encountered Gulshan, her childhood sweetheart. "Gulshan, how are you?" she inquired, her heart fluttering at the sight of him. With a warm smile, Gulshan responded, "How could I marry anyone else?" Embracing tightly, they reunited after years of separation since their school days. Just then, Avira's phone rang—it was Malik. "How was your Bengali New Year's gift?" he inquired his voice a mixture of reassurance and authority. "We look after our own, and you are one of our brightest stars." Malik reminded her of their clandestine role in the country's defense, a hidden force known only to their organization. "Start anew with Gulshan," Malik instructed, his tone softening. "Leave behind the missions and the past. Enjoy this fresh start together, but remember, no contact, or I will assign you another mission." As the call ended, Avira's thoughts lingered on Malik, until she realized Gulshan was no longer beside her. Searching frantically, she found him on one knee, presenting her with a diamond ring. At that moment, Avira knew there could be no better start to the new year than this—starting afresh with the love of her life. Make it more meaningful and ensure marriage topic does not come up immediately after how are you?

ChatGPT

ChatGPT

"Avira," Gulshan's voice was filled with warmth as he enveloped her in a gentle embrace, "I've thought of you every day since we parted."

Tears welled up in Avira's eyes as she held onto Gulshan, feeling a rush of emotions flooding back from their shared past.

"Gulshan, it's been so long," she whispered, her voice trembling with emotion. "I've missed you more than words can express."

Their reunion felt like a balm to Avira's weary soul, a beacon of hope amidst the chaos of her life dictated by Malik's orders.

As they sat together in the dimly lit corner of the bar, reminiscing about their childhood adventures and dreams, Avira found herself yearning for a future where she could be with Gulshan without the shadows of her past haunting her every step.

But just as she began to dare to hope for a life free from Malik's influence, her phone rang, interrupting their tender moment.

Avira's heart sank as she saw Malik's name flashing on the screen, a stark reminder of the web of obligations and secrets that entangled her.

Answering the call, Avira listened to Malik's instructions with a heavy heart, knowing that her newfound happiness with Gulshan was once again at risk of being torn apart by the demands of her clandestine life.

But as the call ended and Avira turned to Gulshan, she found him gazing at her with unwavering determination, his love shining brightly in his eyes.

"Avira," Gulshan spoke softly, taking her hand in his, "whatever challenges lie ahead, I will stand by you. Together, we can overcome anything."

In that moment, Avira realized that with Gulshan by her side, she had the strength to break free from the shackles of her past and embrace a future filled with love, trust, and the promise of a new beginning.

XLII

Rabindra Jayanti

In the early hours of a bright, sunny morning, Arjun turned to his son Avik and asked, "Can you tell me what special day it is today?"

Avik responded promptly, "It's Wednesday, and it's just 2 more days until my summer vacation."

Arjun's voice rose in exasperation as he turned to Soma, "Soma, you haven't informed Avik that today is Rabindra Jayanti—the birth anniversary of the world's greatest Bengali poet."

Soma retorted, "Avik is your son too, Arjun!"

Arjun sighed and turned back to Avik, "Son, have you ever read any stories or poems by Kobiguru?"

Avik confessed, "No, I've heard of Monali Thakur, but not the one you mentioned."

Arjun's frustration manifested as he slammed his hand on the table, "How can you dismiss him as 'the other one'?"

Dressed in a resplendent red saree with a large bindi, Soma joined the father-son literary discussion. Arjun pointed out, "Look, your mom is all dressed up for Rabindra Jayanti, and yet you don't know about Rabindranath Tagore. We Bengalis, especially those from Kolkata, are the custodians of India's rich cultural heritage, including the works of Rabindranath Tagore, who penned our National Anthem. It pains me to think that I couldn't instill in you the values passed down by our parents and Soma's parents."

Avik's response brought a smile to Soma's face, "Wait... are you talking about Rabindranath Tagore? I'm a big fan of his books, and they're even part of my curriculum. I love the song 'Piyu Bole,' which is inspired by his words, as I heard in an interview with Santanu Moitra."

Arjun's heart warmed at his son's revelation, realizing the depth of Avik's understanding. Soma chimed in, "It's all there, dear husband. Times have changed, and so has the form of cultural appreciation. And you'll be pleased to know that Avik is starring in a play called 'Rajarshi' by Rabindranath Tagore, playing the lead role."

XLIII

Children's Day

The onsite coordinator paid a visit to the offshore office during his vacation, a gesture customary for fostering camaraderie. True to tradition, he arrived bearing chocolates for the offshore team, coincidentally aligning with the celebration of Children's Day.

The moment the packet of chocolates was opened, a flurry of excitement ensued as eager hands eagerly reached for the sweet treats. Aman, observing from his cubicle, watched as the chocolates disappeared in a matter of moments. Though someone kindly shared a piece with him, Aman couldn't help but feel a pang of nostalgia.

Memories flooded back to Aman of his school days, when each of his class teachers would gift him a single wafer of chocolate on Children's Day. He couldn't help but reminisce about the simple joy of those moments and how the taste of those wafer chocolates lingered sweeter in his memory than the imported confections now before him.

In that fleeting moment, Aman realized that perhaps his childhood wish to remain forever young and carefree might have been left unfulfilled in the rush to grow up and embrace adulthood.

XLIV

Pratham Expense

Today marked Rohan's inaugural Salary Day, a milestone he eagerly anticipated. Upon receiving the auspicious message on his mobile device, he wasted no time, rushing to the nearest ATM to withdraw a modest sum.

However, instead of heading straight home as one might expect, Rohan veered towards a familiar makeshift shop nestled along the roadside.

There, amidst the morning bustle, he found Ratan, the shop owner, diligently tidying up the accumulated dust.

Upon spotting Rohan, Ratan inquired if he needed anything. To which Rohan responded, "I came to return your money and talk to you"

Perplexed, Ratan couldn't recall any outstanding debts, prompting Rohan to recount a long-forgotten incident from his school days. He confessed to pilfering a toy car from Ratan's shop, expecting reprimand but receiving compassion instead.

Ratan's sage advice resonated deeply with Rohan: "Don't ever steal, son. Return it to me when you accomplish something in life." Moved by the memory, Rohan vowed to repay his debt, not by borrowing from his family but with his own hard-earned money.

With tears welling in his eyes, Ratan struggled to recall the incident, but the sentiment was unmistakable.

Sharing his joyous news, Rohan revealed his recent employment at a pharmaceutical company after graduating with a B. Pharm. He handed Ratan the sum owed, a humble 500 rupees.

Ratan, true to his generous nature, inquired about interest. But Rohan, taken aback, stumbled over his words.

In a heartwarming twist, Ratan suggested they share a cup of tea as his interest—proof that some debts are best repaid with kindness and camaraderie.

And so, Rohan's inaugural salary found its purpose in the unlikeliest of places—a roadside shop and the enduring bond between a young man and the wise shopkeeper who shaped his values.

Navigating Life's Spectrum

XLV

A short Black and White Letter

Dear Friends,

Belated Happy Valentine's Day to you all!

Apologies for the delay in sending this message.

Let's take a moment to share our love story.

I am the blackboard, and my partner is the chalk. Despite our contrasting appearances—I am dark, while he is fair—we've never let such superficial differences cloud our relationship. We firmly believe in equality and reject any form of discrimination.

He stands tall, slender, and handsome, while I am more robust in stature. Yet, the thought of hitting the gym has never crossed our minds. We embrace ourselves just the way we are.

You'll often find us gracing the halls of educational institutions, where students hold us in high regard with affection and admiration. As a pair, we complement each other perfectly, and we hold a deep respect for one another.

He often reminds me, "My height and fair complexion would mean nothing without your presence." Our partnership extends beyond mere aesthetics; together, we play a vital role in guiding children through their first lessons in education.

It's because of us that you're able to read this post seamlessly. In an age dominated by PowerPoint presentations, we continue to hold our ground, providing the foundation for basic education with our timeless utility.

Let's remember to celebrate love every day, not just on a designated date.

With warmest regards and boundless affection,

Yours Lovingly,

Blackboard and Chalk

(The World's most cherished couple for generations)

XLVI
A Letter

Dear Baba,

I hope this message finds you well. How is Maa doing?

Here, I'm doing fine, embracing and celebrating womanhood.

The atmosphere here isn't as warm as back home, but I've come to appreciate the straightforwardness of people.

It's been six months, and I haven't heard your comforting voice saying, "Love you Beta..."

My little sissy, Priya remains in touch with our mom, and she mentioned that you've withdrawn the case.

Honestly, I believe you made the right decision. There's no use prolonging the legal battle.

Oh, and I wanted to share something with you. I've been setting aside a little money, penny by penny, in a small bag in the first drawer of the cupboard in our dining room. This was meant to be a birthday gift for you, my attempt to save on transportation costs to deliver it in person. Please collect it at your convenience. I regret not being able to give it to you personally, but circumstances, as you know, prevented it.

Please convey to Priya that she's welcome to have all my dresses and my share of love from you and Maa. I've moved past any feelings of jealousy; it's simply part of my destiny.

I still vividly remember the pride you felt when I topped my class XII boards. But those same memories are tinged with the pain of the night you disowned me.

I was assaulted and coerced by four intoxicated men. Was it my fault? I pleaded for your support that night, but you remained silent. I understand Maa wasn't in favor of abandoning me, but financial constraints forced her hand. I needed your care and protection, as you were the first man to love me unconditionally.

That fateful night, when I was cast out, I encountered a man who offered me a job. Little did I know the nature of that job...

Do you remember Sharma uncle? He recently visited us. It's the same neighborhood where he resides, the same society that fueled your decision to abandon me. And now, fate has brought him back to prey on me and my coworkers.

I realize I'm dead to you, but I want you to know that I still harbor love for you. Please shield Priya from any similar horrors; she lacks the strength to endure such trials. Truthfully, I'm not sure I possess that strength myself, but I manage to soldier on.

On a brighter note, I've enrolled in daytime classes to complete my graduation. Rest assured, I won't use your surname; I go by the name Sharmila now. Initially, I was silent, grappling with the trauma of my circumstances. But things have settled, and my education has made me a sought-after individual.

Lastly, I request that you burn my diary. It contains dreams and aspirations that you will never be a part of.

Despite everything, I still love you, Maa, and Priya, with you holding the most significant place in my heart.

Your disowned daughter, now known as Sharmila.

XLVII

2 minutes

"I'll call you back in 2 minutes," Sumit replied to a call from Kavya, but those 2 minutes stretched into hours.

Late in the evening, Sumit's phone rang once more, but this time it was from Kavya's mother.

"Kavya has decided to stay with us from now on, and a divorce notice will be filed and sent to you soon. We always wanted the best for Kavya in marriage. Now, she has realized that it's not with you."

Anxious, Sumit questioned, "Not calling in 2 minutes led to a divorce? Are you serious? Where is Kavya now?"

"We're at your apartment and will be leaving soon," came the reply, followed by the tone of a disconnected call echoing in Sumit's ears.

Sumit quickly canceled all his "urgent" scheduled calls for the evening and rushed back home.

Upon arriving home, he was met with pin-drop silence.

As he stepped into his bedroom, he was taken aback by all his family members wishing him a "Happy Birthday." Sumit exclaimed, "Oh! It's my birthday party, and I completely forgot that today is February 22nd."

His heart was racing, trying to adjust to the sudden turn of events.

Kavya burst into laughter, her face filled with joy, "In 2 minutes, you can make Maggi and lose your life too. Stupid!!"

Sumit hugged Kavya tightly in front of everyone, grateful to have her back 'once again' in his life. It remained one of the most memorable birthdays for Sumit.

XLVIII

Ganesan

Ganesan is a person of robust appetite, affectionately described as "slightly" healthy, who takes immense pleasure in indulging in good food.

His family's pantry, brimming with assorted packs of food, is a testament to his deep-rooted love for culinary delights. Yet, Ganesan's affection for food extends beyond mere personal consumption. He finds joy in sharing his passion with others, often hosting treats and gatherings for various occasions or even for trivial reasons.

An exemplary act of his generosity is witnessed in his routine practice of feeding street children after office hours, reflecting his compassion and altruism.

Curious about his profound dedication to food, I once inquired, "What satisfaction do you derive from allocating a significant portion of your salary towards food expenses?"

His response was emphatic, "Money may be allocated to various endeavors, but investing in food transcends mere expenditure. It is a tangible reward for our hard work and sustenance."

To all fellow food enthusiasts, whether they possess a family pack or not, Ganesan extends a heartfelt message: "Eat and extend a helping hand to ensure others can also enjoy the simple pleasure of a good meal."

XLIX

GPS Redefined

Today, Sayeed found himself needing to visit Chandernagar, Kolkata to see his sister, recently discharged from the hospital after recovering from malaria. Opting for a change of pace, he decided to embark on the journey via train, a mode of transportation unfamiliar to him.

As many familiar with Kolkata can attest, navigating the city often requires little more than a sense of direction, as the helpfulness of its citizens tends to fill in the gaps.

Sayeed encountered this firsthand today when he met an elderly individual who generously altered their plans to escort him to the Bally railway station, ensuring he found his way without difficulty.

Despite the heavy rain and his lack of an umbrella prompting a mild scolding from his newfound companion, Sayeed arrived safely at his destination, Chandernagar, thanks to the guidance and assistance of a fellow passenger.

In an era dominated by GPS technology and digital navigation aids, experiences like Sayeed's serve as a reminder of the value of human connection and assistance. Amidst the convenience of modern tools, there remains an irreplaceable significance to the human touch and the camaraderie of fellow travelers.

L
Admin

A few minutes ago, Amit, a professional working in a bank, received a call from an unfamiliar number.

The voice on the other end inquired, "This is Pallavi from a consultancy firm. Are you considering a job change?"

Responding in the customary tone, Amit replied, "Certainly, if it aligns with my skills and profile."

Pallavi continued, "The position we have in mind is for dynamic leaders, a critical managerial role."

Intrigued, Amit expressed interest, asking for further details.

Pallavi elaborated, "We're seeking Social Media Managers for platforms like WhatsApp and Facebook. Your role would involve virtual administration of multiple groups, ensuring cohesion and maintaining group integrity."

Amit was taken aback, questioning the legitimacy of such a job role. "Are you serious? How is this a managerial position?"

Pallavi countered, "Can't one work for the well-being of individuals and still be compensated?"

Expressing his disinterest, Amit explained his aversion to social groups and nonsensical messages.

Pallavi responded, "In an era where joint families are a thing of the past, can't you at least stay connected to a simple WhatsApp group?"

After a brief silence, Pallavi continued, this time revealing her true identity as Amit's cousin, Hiya.

She shared heartfelt sentiments about the significance of family groups, highlighting how they serve as a vital link to loved ones scattered across the globe. Hiya emphasized the value of staying connected and reliving cherished memories through shared updates and photographs.

Amit, moved by her words, apologized and expressed his willingness to join the family group.

Hiya, now revealing herself, added Amit to the group and appointed him as an admin, entrusting him with the responsibility of maintaining its integrity.

Amit, filled with gratitude, expressed his love and appreciation for his sister, promising to embrace his new role wholeheartedly.

LI
Confused!!

In the bustling streets of Kolkata, Ratan's story unfolded, a tale of resilience, love, and unexpected twists that could rival any Bollywood drama.

As a young plumber, Ratan carried not just the tools of his trade, but also the weight of his mother's dreams after his father's passing. Despite his struggles academically, he harbored lofty ambitions of success, fueled by the stories of those bright students who seemed to effortlessly conquer the world.

But life had other plans for Ratan. Graduating with a third division in his 10th exams, he found himself apprenticing under the wing of Jhontu Da, a seasoned plumber. Tragedy struck once more when his mother passed away, leaving Ratan feeling adrift in a sea of loneliness.

Amid his despair, fate threw Ratan a curveball in the form of Tumpa, the sister of his mentor. Their bond blossomed into a tentative romance, with Tumpa even considering leaving her husband for Ratan. However, destiny had a different script in mind, as Tumpa's husband managed to win her back with promises of change.

Alone once more, Ratan found himself grappling with routine until a glimmer of hope appeared in the form of a lottery ticket. The prospect of a life-changing sum beckoned him, but tragedy struck when Ratan met his end in a fatal accident, lost in thoughts of Tumpa.

But fate wasn't done with Ratan yet. As a ghost condemned to wander, he learned of his posthumous lottery win, a staggering Rs. 1 crore. Determined to share his newfound wealth with Tumpa, Ratan's spectral form sought her out, only to be met with an unexpected willingness on her part to marry him.

As Ratan navigates this surreal twist of fate, he finds himself besieged by former crushes vying for his affection, adding to the confusion of his afterlife. In this whirlwind of events, Ratan turns to you, the readers, seeking guidance on how to make sense of this newfound complexity.

Amidst the backdrop of Kolkata's bustling streets, Ratan's journey unfolds, a captivating tale of love, loss, and the mysteries of the afterlife that will leave you spellbound till the very end.

LII

Blood Color

Abhay once again finds himself at Preety's house today, continuing a tradition that began during their college days—a tradition of celebrating Raksha Bandhan together. It all started when Preety expressed her longing for a brother to tie the Rakhi, and from that day forward, this sweet ceremony has endured.

Now, after 40 years, neither Abhay nor Preety have forgotten this special day, despite the passage of time and the establishment of their own families. Even with grandchildren of their own, they still uphold this cherished tradition.

Sometimes, the bonds formed through shared experiences and emotions surpass those of blood relations. It's a testament to the enduring warmth and connection they share, proving that relationships are defined not just by blood ties, but by the depth of feeling and mutual care.

Indeed, the essence of Raksha Bandhan lies not solely in the colors of the thread, but in the sentiments and affection that bind hearts together.

LIII

Teacher

Miss Pallabi Sarkar is a dedicated high school Physics teacher at St. Agnes School, whose unwavering commitment to her students has defined her career since her graduation. Living with her mother, she has devoted her entire life to nurturing young minds.

Miss Sarkar's impact extends far beyond the classroom. She has tirelessly offered extra classes after school, providing invaluable support to students without ever seeking compensation for private tuition.

One such student is Sujay, now settled in Washington D.C. and employed at NASA. Reflecting on his journey, Sujay recalls the pivotal role Miss Pallabi played during his early years. Coming from a financially constrained family, he remembers the distress of being unable to afford school fees, which threatened his ability to take the ICSE exams. It was Miss Pallabi who intervened, using her salary to settle his debts and ensure he could continue his education.

Sujay's gratitude knows no bounds. With Miss Pallabi's unwavering support, he went on to achieve the second rank in his school, setting the stage for a bright future. Even during his college years, Miss Pallabi continued to be a guiding force, offering assistance whenever needed.

Whenever Sujay returns to Kolkata, visiting his teacher is a non-negotiable priority. For him, Miss Pallabi isn't just a teacher; she is the embodiment of purpose and inspiration in his life.

In their weekend conversations, Sujay learns about the countless other students whose lives Miss Pallabi has touched. Her dedication to nurturing dreams and overcoming obstacles alongside her students remains undiminished.

Miss Pallabi's ongoing advocacy for her students' aspirations serves as a testament to her enduring commitment to their success. Through her unwavering support and tireless advocacy, she continues to be a beacon of hope for countless students like Sujay, shaping lives and inspiring futures.

LIV
Photo stories

Karan gazes at the smiling photograph of Shanaya, a snapshot captured by his hand. Memories flood back of the disagreement they once had over purchasing a DSLR camera.

Like many IT professionals, Karan dabbled in various hobbies, from learning the guitar after watching "Rock On" to experimenting with the mouth organ inspired by a song from "Hemlock Society." However, it was watching Ranbir Kapoor in "Wake Up Sid" that ignited his passion for photography.

Despite initial reluctance, Karan eventually acquired the DSLR, driven by an insatiable desire to pursue his newfound interest. The first radiant image he captured of Shanaya still graces his laptop's wallpaper, a cherished keepsake from a bygone era.

Tragically, Shanaya's life was cut short by a miscarriage, leaving Karan to cherish this amateurish yet profoundly meaningful photograph as a constant companion in his life.

In the poignant reality of loss, Karan finds solace in the power of a single memory captured in a photograph, evoking a myriad of emotions and preserving cherished moments that transcend time.

Indeed, it is often a solitary memory that can evoke countless images, and sometimes, a single photograph holds within it a lifetime of memories.

LV

Saina

Saina, a young professional from a conservative background, revels in the freedom of exploring life's adventures, whether it's strolling in shorts or indulging in typical mid-20s pursuits.

Her journey through love and companionship took unexpected turns, from a disillusioning online romance to a casual yet comforting connection with a CAT aspirant. While she never envisioned a future with him, she cherished his company.

As fate would have it, the CAT aspirant found success and moved on to an IIM, leaving Saina alone among her circle of friends. Amidst frequent heartbreaks, there was always one person who stood by her side, offering unwavering support.

Friendship blossomed between them, a bond that transcended romantic entanglements. Though they never crossed the line into a romantic relationship, their connection remained strong, untouched by the label of a breakup.

Now on the brink of marriage, Saina grapples with the fear of losing this cherished friendship. Despite her impending nuptials, she is reluctant to let go of the comfort and familiarity their bond provides.

In the tapestry of her life, Saina understands that sometimes it's the memories shared and the companionship experienced that holds the greatest significance, regardless of whether they are bound by the ties of togetherness.

LVI

Agreement

In the wake of the e-commerce revolution, expenses have skyrocketed for users across the board. Enter Karan and Jui, a married couple navigating the challenges of budgeting amidst the allure of online shopping extravaganzas like "Big Zillion Days," "Big Fashion Week," and "Dil-Deal."

As their income struggles to keep pace with their burgeoning expenses, Karan feels the pressure of unnecessary spending spurred on by enticing offers. Concerned about their financial well-being, he suggests to Jui that they revert to their pre-online shopping habits, opting to purchase items offline as they had done before.

Though initially hesitant, Jui reluctantly agrees to Karan's proposal, recognizing the need to curb their spending. This decision prompts further adjustments, including Jui's decree to remove sports channels from their TV subscription packages. Despite Karan's objections, Jui remains steadfast, prioritizing financial prudence over her husband's sports fandom.

In the aftermath of these agreements, Karan turns to the internet to satisfy his sports cravings, while Jui finds solace in traditional shopping outings at month's end. While their spending decreases, Karan must endure the intellectual rigors of daily soap operas, a small price to pay for financial stability.

Ultimately, their compromise results in a reduction in both sports consumption and online shopping, leading to a more balanced approach to household finances.

LVII
Navigating Bonds

Rohit and Priyanka, childhood sweethearts, found themselves ready to tie the knot after establishing their careers in IT. Convincing their parents was no small feat, especially given Priyanka's father's initial reluctance. However, with time, he came around to the idea of their union.

Amidst the wedding preparations, an unintentional remark from Rohit inadvertently reopened old wounds. When Priyanka mentioned her father's desire for some quality time before the wedding, Rohit made a thoughtless comment about her father's initial objections to their relationship.

Priyanka's reaction was swift and fierce. Defending her father, she reminded Rohit of the hurtful moments they had endured. Feeling defensive, Rohit attempted to lighten the mood, but Priyanka made it clear that her father's place in her life was non-negotiable.

Realizing his mistake, Rohit apologized, expressing his love and respect for Priyanka's father. Their banter turned playful as they joked about their relationship dynamics, finding solace and laughter in each other's company.

Ultimately, their exchange highlighted the importance of understanding and respecting each other's family bonds, even in moments of disagreement or tension.

LVIII
Onsite

Rohit, a software engineer who settled in the US, pursued his master's degree at New York University and currently resides in Philadelphia. Aman, a close friend and ally of Rohit, often joins him for weekend outings.

One weekend, as they were heading to a restaurant for dinner, they encountered an unexpected confrontation from a stranger who questioned their presence in the country and accused them of taking away jobs from locals.

Rohit, unfazed by the stranger's hostility, calmly asserted that job opportunities should be based on merit and qualifications rather than nationality. Aman, sensing the tension, urged Rohit to ignore the stranger's remarks and move on.

Undeterred, the stranger persisted in his accusations until Rohit challenged him to reconsider his perspective. Rohit emphasized the importance of education and offered his assistance to the stranger in pursuing further schooling to improve his prospects.

In a surprising turn of events, the stranger, later identified as Michael, acknowledged his mistake and expressed gratitude for the offer of help. With Rohit and Aman's guidance, Michael embarked on a journey to better himself, eventually earning a degree in technology and securing an onsite assignment in India.

This encounter serves as a reminder of the transformative power of education and compassion, demonstrating how a willingness to extend a helping hand can change lives for the better.

LIX

Silent Wish

Terrence and Shabana shared a dream of eternal togetherness, but their families had different plans. Despite their deep love, they were forced to part ways.

Years later, Terrence succumbed to cancer, a fact kept hidden from Shabana. Unbeknownst to her, she experienced a growing unease in her behavior and thoughts. Tragically, pneumonia claimed her life in the same year.

In death, they found the unity they were denied in life. Their graves lie side by side, fulfilling their silent wish to be together forever.

Their story is a poignant reminder of the power of love, even in the face of adversity and separation.

LX

2nd Innings

As Amit escorted his mother into the 2nd Innings House, he couldn't shake off the feeling that the caretaker recognized her. Engaging in a conversation, the caretaker inquired about her presence there, revealing that she was Amit's stepmother. It came to light that in the past, the caretaker had suggested placing Amit in an orphanage to start afresh, but Amit's mother had adamantly refused, feeling ill-equipped to provide him with proper care and attention.

Life had taken a drastic turn after the passing of Amit's father, further complicated by significant changes following Amit's marriage. The caretaker couldn't help but express a sense of regret, suggesting that things might have turned out differently had Amit's mother listened to her advice. Despite the implications, Amit's mother offered only a blank smile in response.

The realization hit Amit hard, stirring a whirlwind of emotions within him. He felt the ground beneath him tremble as he sought forgiveness, overwhelmed by the weight of the situation. Despite his earnest desire to take her home, his mother chose to remain in the 2nd Innings House, resigned to her solitude.

The poignant tale serves as a reminder of the enduring consequences of past decisions and the elusive nature of redemption. Despite Amit's attempts to make amends, the rift caused by lost love and respect seemed irreparable, leaving his mother to face her twilight years alone.

LXI

Interesting

He was once described as terribly unromantic, boring, and often careless, lost in the labyrinth of his thoughts. These traits ultimately led to the dissolution of his 10-year bond with the girl, mere moments before they were to seal their commitment to marriage.

Years have passed since then, and the girl now resides in Dubai with her NRI husband. Meanwhile, the boy remains single by day, but his nights are a different story, as he engages in fleeting encounters with multiple partners. Surprisingly, his nightly companions find him captivating, drawn to the allure of his conversation, even though it comes at a monetary cost.

In a twist of fate, what was once considered dull and uninteresting has now transformed into a facade of intrigue, fueled by financial transactions that left his nightly companions believing he possesses a captivating charm.

LXII

A New Day

In the tranquil morning of Badu village, nestled on the outskirts of Purulia, the sun cast its radiant glow upon the dew-kissed grass, painting the scene with serenity. The peaceful ambiance was accompanied by the melodic tunes of the morning birds and the familiar voice of Akashvani, resonating from an old radio operated by a gentle elder in his late 60s. He beckoned his wife, Sarala, with a wistful tone, reminiscing, "Sarala, it's been 5 years now..."

Sarala responded with a bittersweet smile, her heart heavy with longing. Their conversation was interrupted by the fleeting presence of a figure hurrying past, barely glimpsed before disappearing .

Reserved in anticipation, a room remained prepared by Sarala—a room for her daughter, Nia. For five years, she had waited patiently, yearning for even the briefest glimpse of her beloved child. The occasional phone call offered little solace to a mother's tender heart, craving the warmth of her daughter's embrace.

Venturing into Nia's room, Sarala's eyes widened in disbelief as she beheld her sleeping daughter. Was it a dream, or perhaps a trick of fading memory? Tentatively, she reached out to touch Nia, confirming her presence with a gentle nudge. Overwhelmed with emotion, Sarala enveloped her daughter in a tight embrace, tears streaming down her weathered cheeks.

Nia stirred from her slumber, reciprocated her mother's embrace, the years of separation melting away in their tearful reunion. Wordlessly, they clung to each other, finding solace in the shared embrace of mother and daughter.

Meanwhile, the elderly gentleman, Sarala's husband, sought his wife's company, his request for tea serving as a mundane distraction from the poignant moment unfolding. Unbeknownst to him, his daughter's return was imminent, a surprise that would stir his soul to its core.

As Nia ventured into the living room, she playfully covered her father's eyes, her presence evoking a mixture of disbelief and joy. With trembling hands, he removed the blindfold to behold his precious daughter standing before him. Overwhelmed by emotion, he enveloped her in a tight embrace, tears of disbelief and gratitude welling in his eyes.

Amidst their tearful reunion, Nia's father reflected on the sacrifices made to ensure her success—the sale of land to finance her education, and the defiance of societal norms to secure her future. Now, with her return as a qualified doctor, the pride in his daughter's achievements eclipsed any doubts or hardships endured.

In the embrace of her parents, Nia found her sanctuary, her resolve unwavering as she expressed her desire to remain by their side. Her love for her family surpassed any aspirations of a lucrative career or societal expectations, embodying the true essence of filial devotion.

As the dawn of a new day illuminated their humble abode, the trio stood united, basking in the warmth of their shared love and unyielding bond—a testament to the triumph of family over adversity.

In this moment of profound reunion, the once-convicted dacoit Raghu's house witnessed a transformation—a symbol of redemption and the enduring power of love.

LXIII

Strange are friends

On the eve of friendship day, I want to share about a friend of mine who is not on Facebook . We meet every single day and he always helps me out during the most critical time of my day . He does not give a pout or click selfies, but always helps us to click photos during any official parties . We discuss the scores of football matches and we have a healthy wordy battle between East Bengal and Mohun Bagan. I feel amazed how a person , whom everyone ignores, has become a friend in a corporate life. His specks are broken and tells me it's the new style. He is not that fashioned as you may say and he doesn't even know that I consider him my friend. He is aged than me and his grey hair suggests his age is somewhat 10 times that of my IT experience. Whenever I with my gang of colleagues come down for lunch , within seconds of waving my hand I see him standing near me to help us.

I remember how depressed I was when I got bad bands and was a rejected candidate for an onsite opportunity. This person came to me and talked for a while , these things matter a lot. Whenever I feel low , I talk to him about anything and I feel good. This Eid, I gifted him a new t-shirt and he was overjoyed about it. He wore it one day and showed everyone his new gift and pointed a finger at me as I was fortunate enough to have given it .

LXIV

Duckworth Lewis Method

Rohit received urgent news of an official assignment that required his immediate departure on Rakhi Day. Ahana, studying in Pune, had meticulously planned to celebrate the occasion with her brother in Mumbai. Learning of his departure over a phone call on Sunday evening, Ahana couldn't suppress her disappointment. "Can't they wait just one more day to send you to South Africa?" she exclaimed in frustration. Rohit, ever the calming presence, reassured her, "It's okay, Ahu. We'll make up for it next year. Let's talk on a video call. By the way, do you know where my passport holder is?" Ahana abruptly ended the call with a resounding "NO," leaving Rohit amused by her sisterly outburst.

Despite being four years younger than Rohit, Ahana was always the more responsible one, especially on Rakhi Day. She never failed to be punctual or forgetful, especially on this special occasion. With heavy hearts, the siblings retired to their respective cities for the night.

In Mumbai, Rohit hurriedly packed his belongings under his mother's guidance. This was his first onsite assignment, and while he was excited, leaving on Rakhi Day filled him with a tinge of sadness. After receiving his parents' blessings, Rohit hailed an auto-rickshaw and set off for the airport.

Meanwhile, Ahana was roused from sleep by the doorbell. To her surprise, a stranger stood at the door, delivering a scooter in her name. Attached was a card that read, "Let the Dhamaka happen right away!!!!" Without hesitation, Ahana dashed to the red scooter, donning the pink helmet.

At the airport, Rohit was completing the final checks on his luggage when his mother informed him of Ahana's unexpected arrival. Confused, Rohit received a call from his sister, who claimed to be standing outside the Mumbai International Airport. Initially skeptical, Rohit turned to see Ahana, clad in pink attire and helmet, waiting eagerly. Despite security restrictions, Ahana's tears and persistence eventually persuaded the guards to allow her entry.

Overwhelmed by his sister's determination, Rohit embraced her tightly as she presented him with a rakhi from a new passport holder. The poignant moment unfolded amidst the bewildered gazes of onlookers, including the mustached security personnel.

As they bid farewell, Rohit departed for his journey, grateful for his sister's unexpected gesture of love and support. Little did anyone know that Ahana was Rohit's step-sister, a bond strengthened not by blood but by unwavering affection and resilience.

LXV
Payback Time

Several years ago, Rajeev and Barkat were neighbors residing in the western parts of India. Both were employed at the same jute mill, earning their livelihoods together. Their days passed contentedly until communal riots erupted in the city, deeply affecting both the Hindu and Muslim communities.

Life took an abrupt turn for all citizens as religious tensions escalated, with each community seeking revenge against the other. Rajeev lived in a Muslim-majority neighborhood, his Hindu household standing alone among many mud-brick homes. Amidst the turmoil, the majority community targeted the minority, seeking retribution for the violence.

Faced with imminent danger, Rajeev packed his family's belongings to flee to safety. Unbeknownst to him, the assailants were aware of his plans and ambushed him and his family. Stranded in their home, Rajeev, his wife Mohona, and their 19-year-old daughter sought refuge in Barkat's house, using a hidden route to reach safety.

Fast forward to the present day...

Floods wreak havoc in the same western region of India, with homes submerged and lives at risk due to rising water levels in the Saraswati River. Desperate villagers flee in search of shelter, food, and clean water, while children fall ill from the lack of basic amenities.

Amid the chaos, one home stands as an unofficial sanctuary for flood-stricken people. A bearded man and a woman in a burqa, seeking refuge from the rain, are welcomed by a young woman. Little do they know, the man recognizes Rajeev, the homeowner, from their past encounter during the riots.

Realizing his past mistake, the man, named Akhtar, seeks forgiveness from Rajeev, who responds with a heartfelt embrace, leaving Akhtar teary-eyed. Barkat, witnessing the reconciliation, smiles with satisfaction. Together, the trio embraces, celebrating the triumph of humanity over past grievances.

As prayers for better weather are offered in the home, a poignant scene unfolds as both Hindu and Muslim rituals are performed in the same space. In this moment, a portrait of India emerges, painted with the colors of diversity and unity, and adorned with the brushstrokes of humanity.

LXVI

Not Okay

She: "You look sad."

He: "No, I'm absolutely fine."

She: "This absolutely just messed up your fineness. What happened? Loan problem?"

He: "No."

She: "Barca lost?"

He: "No."

She: "Official problem?"

He: "No."

She: "Fought with someone?"

He: "No."

She: "Oh no! Is it the onsite issue?"

He: Silent gasping

She: "Come on, yaar. Same old story. Let's go onsite with our own money. Give a damn to onsite and a double damn to the opportunity. Just let's go. You can go there for a mere 4000/-. Let's go."

He: Leaves?

She: ".... your leaves...bind them to your tree. Where was the ethics when you didn't get the onsite opportunity? Just tell them to go to hell and let's book tickets."

He: "But where do we go?"

She: "To the dining room for now... let's eat."

Both genders had dinner and went to sleep, forgetting about the trip. Both were not okay, but more than okay.

LXVII

Bonds Beyond Blood

Once again, Ashtami arrives, casting its golden glow over the bustling streets. Amongst the throngs of devotees, a figure stands out—Meenakshi, resplendent in her finest attire, waits patiently at the corner of the Puja Pandal. Beside her, her husband fidgets, urging her to leave, but Meenakshi remains steadfast in her anticipation.

Suddenly, a familiar face appears, and Meenakshi's eyes light up with recognition. Rushing forward, she envelops Swarnali in a warm embrace. They were classmates at Dum Dum Girls High School forty years ago, and their bond has endured through the sands of time.

In the era of social networking, their annual reunion on Ashtami is a cherished tradition—a testament to the enduring power of friendship. No calls or messages are exchanged, yet they unfailingly meet to offer Pushpanjali together.

Meenakshi reaches for a familiar packet, a token of their tradition, but Swarnali gently refuses, insisting, "Suman is here; you should give it to him yourself." Each year, Meenakshi prepares a gift for Suman, her son settled in the USA. As the mother of a gold medalist student, she treasures Suman like her own, and on this day, she feels the warmth of motherhood once again.

Suman, an IT professional residing in the USA, seldom visits Meenakshi Aunty. Yet, the mere knowledge of his presence in the city brings solace to both mothers, bridging the miles that separate them.

In the end, beneath the veneer of social status, familial ties, and geographical distances, beats the same red blood—the universal bond that unites us all.

LXVIII

Pink

Radhika, resplendent in a pink gown, and Dhruv, dapper in a suit, reunited after 5 years at the College Reunion.

The former lovebirds, now out of touch, exchanged warm greetings with everyone and reminisced about old memories.

Radhika couldn't help but notice that the pattern Dhruv used to unlock his mobile screen was still the letter "R".

Dhruv, lost in thought, recalled his words from years ago, "Radhika, please come to meet me in pink always."

LXIX

Promotion

After completing the necessary paperwork, the middle-aged banker turned to the young customer and asked, "So, as another year approaches, how has 2017 treated you, Champ?"

The customer, affectionately addressed as "Champ," responded, "It's been quite good, Sir. Thankfully, we finally parted ways this year."

The banker, taken aback, inquired, "What? Did you two break up? After being together for 7 long years?"

With a smile and a hint of blush, the young man replied calmly, "Yes, Sir. Finally! This year, we ended our relationship as boyfriend and girlfriend and took the next step by getting married. We've been promoted, Sir..."

LXX

Campusing

"All candidates have been selected from this college, Sir," the junior associate reported, the words resonating in Mr. Sengupta's ears. With a sigh, he eased his body into the cushioned armchair of the Hall room, which had been temporarily transformed into an interview cabin. Closing his eyes, a delightful curve formed on his face as he reminisced about a decade ago when he stood in the same room clutching his testimonials, seeking admission to this very college. He vividly recalled the stark red letters on his application form - "REJECTED."

Suddenly, the Chairman and the Principal of the college entered, acknowledging Mr. Sengupta's support for the institution. "Sir! Thank you for your support to our college. It's our pleasure that you think our students are capable enough to serve your company. Would you like to have anything, tea or coffee?" they asked.

For Mr. Sengupta, this moment was a culmination of achievement, enough to satisfy the heart of the billionaire seated in the comfortable armchair in the Hall.

LXXI

Party

A friend messaged Alok, "Today's weather is perfect for romance. Who would've thought Kolkata could bless us with such soothing weather at the start of the sweltering summer season?"

Alok replied, lifting his head from his book, "Indeed, it's true. But that requires a boyfriend, girlfriend, or in our current age, perhaps a husband or wife."

The friend responded, showing more interest, "You can enjoy it with your group of friends too."

Alok set aside his book and retorted, "So, would you hold your friend's hand and play 'kiss me kiss me' in the park?"

His friend handled it calmly, "So, to enjoy cloudy weather, you need to go hand in hand, don't you? I gave you my hand, see."

Alok joked, "You know, it's similar to Gabbar, 'ye hath mujhe de de'."

To which, his friend replied, "You want my life, I can give that too."

Alok chuckled, "You giving me a treat is enough for me."

"Come over to my place, let's have a party," proclaimed Rajat, Alok's best friend.

LXXII

Safe

"So when can we be safe, Mom?" Lakshmi inquired.

Durga replied, "When men will behave like men!"

The young daughter asked, "So when will they behave like men?"

In a calm tone, the mom replied, "Tell me, from where do they evolve?"

Lakshmi replied, "From a woman..."

Durga smiled profusely, "You got the answer."

LXXIII
Choice

An open discussion forum "Biwiyo ki Baat" was made open for the audience.

There were 3 participants each from different fraternities of the society.

Participant 1: Subhra, wife of an eminent politician

Participant 2: Ratna, Wife of an army personnel.

Participant 3: Urmi, Wife of an accused terrorist.

Subhra: "Why even we are sitting with a terrorist's wife."

Urmi: "Can you please get your stats correct? My husband is just a convict and it's not proved yet."

Ratna: "I think there is enough pieces of evidence for his arrest."

Urmi: "Power speaks for itself."

Ratna: "A convict is a convict. He must have done something which you are not aware of."

Urmi: "I am sure my husband will come out clean. He is my hero."

Ratna: "Oh please, a terrorist can never be a hero.!!!"

Subhra laughed loudly in appreciation of the statement made by Ratna.

Urmi: "So do you think a tainted politician immersed in innumerable criminal bookings is a hero . An army personnel who takes money from outsiders to infiltrate our country is a hero?"

Ratna and Subhra chorused: "Do you have any proof?"

Urmi : "Exactly that's what my point is!"

Ratna replied spontaneously,"My husband is a hero and I don't need your consent to get it right".

As it was said,"Greater power comes with greater responsibilities but unfortunately here greater power comes with greater misuse",replied Urmi.

Subhra: "I think we are in the wrong company...!"

Urmi said, "So, who is a hero? A person who is accused of multiple scams or a person who helps infiltration?? Ladies, please reply".

Urmi continued,"Do we really need these heroes in our country?."

Urmi asked the other two ladies,"Who is a hero?"

Ratna said,"A hero is a person who saves the country and keeps its citizen safe just like my husband does?".

Urmi continued, "At the cost of infiltration?

Subhra said, "A hero is a person who works day in and day out to keep the citizens happy and so that basic amenities are provided.

Urmi: "At the cost of corruption."

She went on

"At the same time,a professor who was peacefully protesting against the wrongdoings of the government is termed as a terrorist and anti-national . I can't conclude that he is innocent but the action is done at the cost of humanity"

The choice is yours Who will you choose ahead of others?

LXXIV

Did anything happen?

The office was peaceful on that bright July day, despite the rain outside.

Avik praised his team, saying, "You guys did a great job. I'm really proud of you."

Someone grumbled, "But it doesn't show up in our paychecks."

Avik joked, "Well, since our work went well and was appreciated, let's celebrate, shall we?"

So, the team decided to have a party, with Avik covering the costs.

But amid the fun, Avik's phone rang with a familiar ringtone in Hindi, "What happened...how did it happen...(Ye Kya hua!!) "

Despite the laughter at the ringtone choice, Avik's face turned red with worry.

He took the call and grew serious as he learned of a problem reported by the Manager. Frustrated, he demanded answers, singling out the developer responsible for a key report.

When Shalini, the developer, couldn't be found, Avik's anxiety spiked. He received a message from her, explaining her absence due to family issues.

Feeling overwhelmed, Avik confided in Rohit, who reassured him and helped look into the problem despite their different roles.

After a thorough investigation and working with the user, Rohit found a solution and successfully implemented it.

The quick fix impressed the client, showing the team's resilience even without Shalini.

Later that evening, Shalini reached out, sharing her happy news of marriage and thanking Avik for his understanding. As she asked about any updates during her absence, the team eagerly awaited her return.

Nothing is impossible if we are backed by a good team.

LXXV
Happy Ending

Raj sighed deeply, reflecting on the passage of time since his breakup with Simran, a decade ago.

He found himself revisiting old email conversations and text messages from that period, no matter how brief they were. Among them, a screenshot of Simran's heartfelt declaration of love still held a special place in his hidden folder.

Today, both Raj and Simran have moved on, building new lives and, perhaps, finding happiness in their respective paths.

Yet, despite the passage of time, the memories of their past relationship lingered on, unchanged.

Their story was not one of the cinematic romance depicted in DDLJ; real life seldom follows such scripted narratives.

Indeed, life's journey doesn't always culminate in a fairy-tale ending, but rather in the complex and unpredictable twists of reality.

Conclusion

After this book, we find ourselves immersed in a tapestry of diverse narratives, each woven with intricacy and emotion. From tales of love and loss to moments of triumph and redemption, these stories capture the essence of the human experience in its myriad forms.

As we journeyed through the pages, we encountered characters grappling with the complexities of life, facing challenges both internal and external. We witnessed their joys and sorrows, their hopes and fears, resonating with the universal truths that bind us all.

Through the laughter and tears, the highs and lows, we were reminded of the power of resilience, the strength of the human spirit, and the enduring capacity for love and compassion.

As we bid farewell to these stories, let us carry with us the lessons they imparted, the insights they offered, and the emotions they evoked. For in the mosaic of life, it is through storytelling that we find solace, understanding, and connection.

May these tales continue to inspire, provoke thought, and ignite the imagination long after the final page is turned. And may they serve as a reminder of the beauty and complexity of the human condition, uniting us in our shared humanity.

Thank you for embarking on this literary journey.